YOU ASKED FOR IT!
WHAT I KNOW ABOUT BOYS,
a sequel to the popular
WHEN SEPTEMBER RETURNS.

"You're busy all day?" I asked incredulously.

"Uh—I think so."

"Well—shall I call you later?" If I hadn't been so sure of how he felt about me, I'd have thought he was trying to get rid of me.

"Uh—I don't think I'll be here."

He was trying to get rid of me! Had he gone home and thought about me and decided that the whole evening had been a mistake, that I wasn't his kind of girl after all? Or had I misread him completely? Was he really a guy who naturally poured on the charm with any girl, without meaning a word of it?

Could I be that wrong about guys?

McCLURE JONES has lived in the Midwest, the South and California. She now considers the Pacific Northwest her home. It is the setting for most of her fiction. She is a graduate of the University of Washington, with a major in English and a minor in teaching. Before becoming a full-time writer, she taught high school and was a free-lance journalist and a magazine editor.

Dear Readers:

Thank you for your many enthusiastic and helpful letters. In the months ahead we will be responding to your suggestions. Just as you have requested, we will be giving you more First Loves from the boy's point of view; and for you younger teens, younger characters. We will be featuring more contemporary, stronger heroines, and will be publishing, again in response to your wishes, more stories with bittersweet endings. Since most of you wanted to know more about our authors, from now on we will be including a short author's biography in the front of every First Love.

For our Book Club members we are publishing a monthly newsletter to keep you abreast of First Love plans and to share inside information about our authors and titles. These are just a few of the exciting ideas that First Love from Silhouette has in store for you.

Nancy Jackson
Senior Editor
Silhouette Books

WHAT I KNOW ABOUT BOYS
McClure Jones

First Love from Silhouette

Published by Silhouette Books New York

America's Publisher of Contemporary Romance

First Loves from Silhouette by McClure Jones

SILHOUETTE BOOKS
300 E. 42nd St., New York, N.Y. 10017
Copyright © 1985 by Diane McClure Jones
Cover artwork copyright © 1985 by Magic Image, Inc.

Distributed by Pocket Books

ISBN: 0-373-06140-4

First Silhouette Books printing May, 1985

10 9 8 7 6 5 4 3 2 1

America's Publisher of Contemporary Romance

Printed in the U.S.A.
RL 5.7, IL age 11 and up

WHAT I KNOW
ABOUT BOYS

1

Let me tell you about boys. They are handsome and clever and exciting and thoughtful and sweet. That's one day. The very next day they are still handsome, but they are also bossy and cranky and thoughtless and rotten.

When I explained that to Marci, she glanced up at me over the edge of the book she was reading and said, "Had a fight with Rick?"

Marci Palmer is my roommate in Smith Hall, the oldest dormitory at the U., and also the only all-women dorm, which is why it is also almost all freshmen, too. We freshmen get last choice on housing.

"He makes me so mad!" I said. "We had a date to go see that movie I've been waiting for all year, and now he says he's got other plans!"

"Other plans?"

"And he waited until this morning at breakfast to tell me in the cafeteria!"

"What sort of other plans?" she asked.

"He said he needed to work in the computer room and he'd reserved time for tonight! Can you believe that!"

"Maybe he has a paper due," Marci said. That's Marci. She's always so calm and sensible, and she always thinks of things like assignments first.

"Marci," I said, trying to keep my voice very calm and level, because, honestly, I did not need my roommate and best friend taking the side of my rotten boyfriend, "the point is, he promised. And today he said he didn't remember promising."

Marci said, "If you still want to go to the movie, I'll go with you, Greta."

"I don't care about the movie!"

"Then why are you upset?"

"I'm not upset!" I shouted.

Marci is thin and pretty, with high cheekbones and very dark eyes and wavy dark brown hair. If she would wear makeup, she'd look like a model, but she's more interested in getting good grades than she is in being beautiful. If I didn't like her so much, she'd drive me crazy, the way she sees right through me.

She said, "Then why are you collecting all your shower stuff?"

I hadn't even noticed that I was, but while I'd been talking, I'd been gathering my towel and robe and shampoo and soap and skin moisturizer and hair conditioner and washcloth and sponge and back brush and some other stuff. Looking down at what I was holding in my hands, I said, "I'm going to take a shower."

"You took a shower before you went to breakfast. That was only two hours ago."

Our eyes met and I started to giggle. Marci grinned. She was right, as usual. Whenever I'm upset, I go stand in a hot shower until I feel better, and considering how often I've been upset since I started dating Rick, it's a miracle that my skin hasn't dried up and washed away down the drain.

Grabbing her backpack and hanging it over her shoulder, Marci headed for the door. "Gotta run, or I'll be late for my nine o'clock."

"See you later," I said.

She paused outside the door to turn and say, "Greta, don't get too upset about Rick. You know he'll be in a better mood in a day or two."

"I know," I said.

She closed the door and left me alone with my armload of shower stuff that I didn't need because, although I was upset, I wasn't going to let that rotten Rick Blair drive me to taking showers every two hours.

It is important—no, more than that—it is imperative that a girl not let a boy's behavior cloud her judgment. I read that in a magazine and as soon as I saw it, I knew it was a piece of advice meant especially for me, so I cut it out and pinned it to the bulletin board above my desk. And I reread it every now and then, and believed it so completely that I often repeated the advice to the other girls in the dorm.

So why did I let Rick Blair absolutely blot out every bit of common sense I'd ever had?

Let me tell you about Rick. He is tall and very dark, with thick hair and a beard and sharp bones that would photograph beautifully, like some TV star, complete with an arched nose and wide brows and incredible black eyes; and when he wants, he has a fabulous smile, but he doesn't smile all that much. Anyway, everybody says we look terrific together, because I am tall and blond and blue-eyed. Now that is a terrible reason to date a boy, and I'd be the first one to say so to anyone, and it is definitely not why I date Rick.

I date Rick because the first time I saw him I thought he was the most gorgeous guy I'd ever met, and I couldn't believe it when he noticed me too, and that also is a rotten reason for dating a guy and not one I'd recommend to anyone, but I give better advice than I follow.

So there it is. The reason I date Rick is because I am crazy about him. And when he wants to be, he can be as sweet as he is handsome.

When I left home last fall to come to the U. and live in a dorm, it was the first time I'd ever been away from home for more than a week or so at a time. Though I wouldn't have admitted it to anyone, ever, I was shaking hard after my parents had helped me unload my gear, and hugged me good-bye. When they left me standing alone on the front steps of the dorm, waving as their car pulled away from the curb, I had to grit my teeth and dig my nails into my palms to keep from running after them, shouting for them to come back for me.

Not that I didn't want to go away to college. Of course I did. But wanting to do something and feeling completely confident about it are not the same thing. I graduated young from high school. I was only seventeen last fall when I started college. It occurred to me, way back home in my small town last summer, that although I'd done a fair amount of dating in high school, college boys were going to be different. They'd probably all be sophisticated, much too adult to notice me. So I'd spent the summer reading all the fashion magazines, especially the ones written for college girls, and I devoured all their advice articles and columns.

I learned all the tricks for using makeup and a blow-dryer. I won't even tell you how many days I spent scrubbing off my face and starting over again. And I used only half my clothing allowance to buy my school clothes and kept the other half so that I'd have money to buy whatever was the right thing to wear at the U., in case it turned out that my clothes were not what everyone was wearing, which one of the articles said to do. I made lists of how to judge a boy's character from his behavior. I made more lists of how to handle various dating situations.

If I'd ever put that much effort into my homework, I probably would have been a valedictorian or something.

By September I was feeling superconfident and ready to shine, and then on the trip my confidence started to shrivel, and the more my folks chattered away about what a wonderful opportunity college was, the less sure I felt. But I think I'd have been all right if my mother hadn't surprised me by opening a box that I hadn't remembered packing and pulling out my old Holly Hobbie spread and making up my bed in my new room in the dorm. And then she arranged my desk.

Who would have believed that my mom still had my Dumbo elephant bookends, which I think someone gave me when I was eight years old and that I'd tossed in the attic by the time I was twelve? And worse yet, why should anything so silly make me feel eight years old again?

So there I stood on the steps, with my lip quivering, almost feeling as though I'd just been dropped off for my first day of kindergarten, when this darling guy rushed up the stairs toward the dorm, paused in front of me, gave me a wide grin of gorgeous white teeth and said, "Hi, there," before continuing on his way.

And before I could turn around or blink or anything, another fantastic guy glanced up at me as he walked by across the lawn and gave me a wink.

I couldn't believe it. I stood there like a mindless robot and slowly turned my head, taking it all in. For the first time I noticed that green lawns ran from the dorm to the street, and they were crisscrossed with paths and walkways and overhung with shining trees, and sunlight glittered off every bright surface. Behind me the ivy rustled in a light breeze against the brick walls, and all around me stretched a new world of grass-scented air, and shiny cars and honking horns and shouting, waving people. My jeans and T-shirt and hairstyle were exactly right, fit in perfectly with the way all the girls I saw were dressed; and more than that, the whole place was swarming with guys: cute guys, plain guys, fabulous guys, some smiling, some waving; and I realized that I was not going to be some horrible misfit, after all.

Right after that I met Rick. He was at an orientation meeting and he slid into the seat next to mine in the theater-auditorium on the top floor of the Student Union building. I was in a back row because I'd taken the wrong turn and gone into the ballroom by mistake and had to go down the curved staircase and run the whole length of the main corridor to find the back stairs that led to the theater, which was why I was late. Rick was late because he never bothered hurrying for anyone, but I found that out later.

That first time I saw him I was so aware of him, after just one glance, that I was afraid he'd hear my heart pounding. I looked away fast, but he was so handsome my eyes kept straying back to his hand, which was resting on the chair arm between us, and I didn't hear a word the speaker said.

After the meeting had been dismissed, but before I'd had a chance to move, this deep, soft, foxy voice said in my ear, "You a freshman?"

"Yes." I nodded.

"Must be all freshmen here," he said.

I looked up at him and straight into his eyes and I almost drowned in them, they were that deep and gorgeous.

"Let's get out of here," he said, and caught my elbow. I sort of floated along beside him, unable to believe that anyone like him could be an ordinary mortal male freshman.

Actually, he wasn't—not a freshman, anyway— and definitely not ordinary. He explained over coffee in the coffee shop on the main floor of the Union building that he was a junior. He'd transferred to the U., which was why he had to go to the orientation meeting. He also said that he hated his major and he was planning to switch, and probably he told me lots more, but I had trouble remembering it, what with trying to remember to smile and nod and be a good listener and also trying to keep my heart from pounding faster every time our eyes met.

It is important not to let a boy know how you feel about him until you know how he feels about you. I knew that without checking back to my magazine articles. So when he said, "I wonder what there is to do around here at night. Want to come along with me and find out?" I knew I shouldn't sound eager.

I said, "I'm not sure. I think I have a dorm meeting."

Instead of asking for my phone number, he shrugged, stood up and walked off, leaving me alone with my half-empty coffee cup and my memorized dating guidelines.

About the time I'd figured I had the rules wrong, he reappeared, pulled out the chair across from me, swung his leg over the back, sat down, leaned his elbows on the formica table top, stared me in the eyes and said, "What's your phone number?"

As you can see, I started out in full control of the situation, saying the right things at the right time. I think I lost control about six hours later, when Rick pulled me into his arms for the first time, to dance, and I'm not sure I ever regained control again— though, honestly, I kept trying.

Throughout the autumn semester Rick and I had this on-off relationship. We'd have a couple of fabulous times together and then we'd have a big fight. By the time I went home for Christmas break, I'd made up my mind to start my New Year's resolutions with swearing off thinking about Rick, that's how far apart we were.

So I came back to the U. in January with all my priorities straight in my mind. I went out on a couple of dates with Jon Austin, this big teddy bear of a guy, the sort who never says a mean word: I had my life under control. I was even getting my class assignments in on time.

And then Rick popped back into my life. He hung around, phoned, told me how marvelous I looked and how much he'd missed me and I ended up going to the Valentine Dance with him and having a dream of a time.

So with all that going on in my life, why was I sitting at my desk by the window on a bright March morning, staring down through the curtain of ivy at the people hurrying past on the walkways? I should have been working on laundry or doing my aerobics or even studying history for tomorrow's test, but there I sat, daydreaming, trying to figure out how my relationship with Rick kept getting so confused.

I was going back over everything he'd said to me that morning, trying to think of a better answer than the one I'd given him, my mind a blur but my half-focused gaze still on the lawn, when I finally realized someone was waving at me. I shook my head to clear my thoughts.

Then I waved back.

Jon grinned and beckoned me to come outside.

After bossy old Rick, Jon was exactly what I needed. I did a quick touch-up of my makeup, fluffed my hair, popped a breath mint in my mouth and ran out of my room and down the stairs, past the front desk, through the heavy outer door and down the steps, just fast enough to look as though I was hurrying and not intentionally keeping him waiting, but not so fast as to mess up my hair.

Maybe that sounds unbelievably conceited, but honestly, I'm not, just the opposite. I know for sure that without my hair I am nothing. I have this thick, fluffy mass of blond hair that is thick and fluffy because I wash and set and blow-dry it every day, and it is my best feature by miles, and I can't imagine anyone ever noticing me for any other reason; so sure, I worry about it.

Early March rains had washed away the last snow. Now the sun shone down through the bare branches of the maples that lined the main walks, making a perfect day, too warm for coats but cold enough for my favorite bulky sweater and my khaki pants.

Jon said, "I thought you had a class now."

"I cut my nine o'clock today," I said.

"Want to go for coffee?" he asked.

I'd had breakfast with Rick, but I'd been so upset, when he broke our date, that I hadn't eaten much. I said sure and we headed across the lawns and through the small clump of woods to the Student Union building, another ivy-draped brick building, but a lot larger than the dorms. It was fronted by an enormous round fountain that I'd never seen turned on, and stone stairs that ran the width of the building, and a row of three sets of double doors set in stone arches—Gothic, I think. Jon held open the door for me. We hurried to the coffee shop, went through the line picking up donuts and coffee and found an empty table among all the crowded ones.

Jon is big, built solid, a hunk type but not a jock. You know by looking at him that if he ever took up weight lifting it would be because he enjoyed lifting weights, not because he wanted to build muscles to impress other people with. He has a wide, friendly, honest face, covered with freckles. He couldn't lie if he tried. For sure he's an exact opposite from Rick and for sure that's exactly what I needed.

He leaned toward me across the table and smiled. "Now what's this about cutting classes? Having trouble with your course?"

I ran my fingertip around the rim of my coffee cup for something to do with my hands. Not looking at him, I said, "No, the class is okay."

"So then what's the big deal problem?"

"What problem?" I asked, still keeping my gaze on my cup.

"Come on, Greta, this is Jon. I can tell you're upset."

His voice was so kind and understanding I practically burst into tears. I said, "It's nothing. I'll be okay."

"Rick giving you a bad time?" he said.

"Oh, Jon!" I looked up at him and tried to put on a big, shiny smile, to convince him that I was okay, but I guess my smile kind of quivered.

"Don't let that guy push you around," Jon said. "You could have any guy on campus. Why waste your time with Rick?"

"I can't help it," I said.

"Uh-huh," he said, and his voice sounded almost as sad as mine.

It wasn't fair. Jon was so nice. Why couldn't I love him instead of Rick? There were times when I got so mad at myself, being so crazy about Rick and suspecting that that was how Jon felt about me. But at least I wasn't ever mean to Jon. I didn't lead him on one day and dump him the next.

I said, "First he's nice and then he's horrid."

"What's he done this time?"

I blinked because I could feel the tears behind my lids, and then I sort of slid my eyes away, not wanting Jon to guess. "Oh, see, he said he'd take me to something tonight and then this morning he said he was going to work in the computer room tonight, and it wasn't anything important, and I didn't care that much about it; but the thing is, when I mentioned that he'd promised to take me out, he said he hadn't, and then he got mad and said I was making stuff up."

"You and Rick don't communicate very well."

"Huh?"

"Greta, maybe he has to work in the computer room. Maybe he has a project due."

"Maybe," I said. "He didn't say that."

"Did you ask?"

"No," I admitted.

Jon gazed at me with this really serious expression and said, "Ask him, Greta. Find out what he's thinking. You two will never get along until you start being more open with each other."

Jon was such a sweetie. And what he said made sense. But if I went chasing after Rick now, telling him I was sorry I'd been upset that he broke a date because I realized his school work came first, Rick would think I was chasing him. He would. He wasn't reasonable and understanding the way Jon was. But I didn't bother saying any of that to Jon. There he was, trying so hard to be helpful and kind, I didn't want to hurt his feelings.

I said, "Hey, that's what I should do. I should ask him. You're right."

As we left the coffee shop, Jon gave me a quick hug, which he always does, and I hugged him back, which I always do, and he said, "Feel better now?"

"I always feel better after I talk to you," I said.

"Then don't cut any more classes or you'll be the one with problems," he said.

"Yes, sir!" I said, and snapped him a salute before heading away from him across campus for my next class.

My eleven o'clock was tennis. I'll admit that I don't like tennis much. I've never been very good at sports, though heaven knows, I try. I fling myself into any game anyone asks me to join, including soccer and Frisbee and canoeing, but I am invariably the one who kicks the ball toward the wrong goal or tips over the canoe.

However, tennis is different. For some reason, people expect it to be played correctly. They get upset when I dash into my partner's territory. I don't know why, but I have a terrible time remembering to stay on my own side. And then there's the scoring, which has nothing to do with logical counting, and I seem to always forget the score. And also there are very fussy restrictions about whether a ball is in or out. Now if I am close enough to the ball to actually hit it, I hit it, because I am so amazed to be there at all, but if the ball is going out a player is supposed to know that and not hit it, only I never do, so then my partner shouts at me.

As a result, I love to hit the ball back and forth with friends who don't care about rules, but I hate taking tennis as a class. In a class, people are absolutely demented on the subject of rules.

However, none of that is the reason I didn't make it to tennis class. I did not cut on purpose. What happened was that I was distracted. Is there anyone who wouldn't be distracted by what happened to me?

I was rushing down the hill below the woods toward the athletic building where I had to change clothes and collect my gear before reporting to the outdoor courts at eleven sharp, and I wasn't sure I was going to make it. Also, I was still thinking about my problems with Rick, and Jon's advice. So as I cut across the footbridge that crosses this funny little stream that's at the bottom of the woods where it opens into the narrow meadow surrounding one of the play fields, I didn't see this guy at all.

He was all scrunched down, sitting on his heels, his chin on his knees, peering into the long grass at the far side of the bridge. He was wearing faded jeans and a khaki sweat shirt. His hair was the same sort of soft, light brown as his tan. I didn't notice all this until afterwards, but I think that's why I didn't see him. He blended in with the tall grass and the dirt path.

I ran right into him, my knee colliding with his shoulder. I couldn't even guess what I'd hit. My mind did a total blackout. All I could think to do was flail my arms, which sent my purse flying off into the undergrowth but didn't do a thing for my balance. As I doubled up, he toppled over, and we ended in a tangle of legs and arms, both of us shouting.

We weren't shouting words, more like grunts and moans. I felt as though I'd been hit by a flying tackle.

Then a voice from under me said, "You okay?"

As I didn't even know where to begin inventory to see if I was okay, I said, "I guess so."

"Then could you get off me?" he asked.

2

Carefully, I pushed myself up, trying not to put my foot in his ribs or my elbow in his eye, but I wasn't entirely successful. As I untangled myself and stood up, he let out some groans.

"Hey, I'm sorry," I said to the back of his head. He was sprawled face down in the grass.

He rolled over slowly and squinted up at me, the sun in his eyes.

"I didn't see you. Let me give you a hand," I said, and held out my hand.

At first I thought he was going to refuse. Probably he thought that anyone clumsy enough to trip over him would also let go of him. But then he reached up, caught my hand and clambered to his feet.

"How about you? You okay?" he asked.

"Oh sure, maybe a bump or two."

"It was my fault," he said.

At that point I should have insisted that I was the klutz, should have been looking where I was going, and so forth. Only he had this funny look on his face, as though he was waiting to see what sort of line I'd come up with. His eyes crinkled at the edges. Was he secretly laughing at me?

I forgot all I knew about being charming on a first meeting and sputtered, "Yeah, it was! What were you doing, anyway, all crouched down like that in the path?"

"You really want to know?" he asked, and before I could reply, he added, "Come here, I'll show you."

As he was still holding onto my hand, I followed him a step or two to the edge of the grass where he knelt down and I knelt beside him.

Letting go of my hand, he pushed aside the grass and pointed to a fiddlehead, which is the first curled shoot of a fern. As they grow wild everywhere, I couldn't think why he found it so interesting.

"I'm keeping a log on them," he said. "I noted the date this one first appeared, and now I'm measuring it every three days to chart its growth."

"Why?"

"For a botany class. I'll do a scale drawing of its development to turn in with my term paper."

"You a botany major?"

"Uh-uh," he said. "I'm an art major. That's why I'm doing the drawings. My papers are always so lousy, I count on my illustrations to get me a decent grade."

"I wish I had a talent," I said. "I can't write and I can't draw and I'm not athletic and oh! my gosh!"

"What's wrong?"

"I'm supposed to be at tennis at eleven!" I jumped up.

He checked his watch. "It's eleven-fourteen now."

"Oh no! That's the second class I've missed today!"

He stood up and gave me a wide grin and said, "You picked a great day to cut."

He was right. The sun was shining, the sky was bright blue, the air smelled like springtime. All around me new leaves on the birch trees rustled in a light March breeze. I could even hear the stream making little gurgling noises under the wooden footbridge.

And right there in front of me, smiling at me, was this supernice guy. I could tell he was supernice because he had all the right looks for supernice, kind of like anybody's brother, average height, average build, soft wavy hair, slightly crooked teeth, a nose that was maybe a tad too short and too wide but fit perfectly in his square face and eyes that were the same light, warm, sunshine brown as his hair.

And he definitely didn't look like the kind of guy who expected every girl he met to fall madly in love with him, like that rotten Rick.

I said, "I'm Greta."

He said, "I'm David."

"It's been nice running into you," I said and we both laughed. I added, "If I'm not going to make it to tennis, I'd better at least head back to my dorm and get my laundry done."

"Uh-huh," he said.

Now I know enough about boys to know that at that point I could have said something about going to lunch early and he probably would have said that was a good idea and tagged along with me, but honestly, no matter how cute he was, I didn't need another guy in my life. So instead I mentioned the laundry. One thing I know for sure about boys, they never offer to help with the laundry. They may ask girls to help them do *their* laundry, pretending they don't even know how to put soap in a machine, but never the other way around.

"See you," I said, waving, and turned and ran back up the path.

When I reached the top of the woods, I turned to glance toward the bridge, expecting to see him standing there watching me. He wasn't. He was crouched down on the far side again, his notebook open, writing something and peering into the grass. Keeping a log on ferns? I'd have to remember that one to tell to Marci.

Back at my dorm I honestly did do my laundry, which was way past due. I maybe had one clean shirt left, and a couple of sweaters, but I was wearing my last pair of khakis. I planned on catching up on my reading assignment for my afternoon lit class.

I sat cross-legged on top of the washing machine while it chug-a-chugged through a load of my sweats and towels. The laundry room was in the basement and it looked like a basement. There were pipes overhead, a few hanging lights and a couple of grimy windows at ceiling height, which was why I had to sit on top of the machine to get enough light to read.

The assignment was an abysmal bore. There were long paragraphs of descriptions of some guy's guilt complexes, really deadly stuff. What with the warm soapy smell rising around me, plus the dim light and the small print, I was battling to stay awake. So when Allison, who lived down the hall from me, wandered in, I was relieved to be interrupted.

"I've got three of the machines going," I said, "but those two on the end are empty and one of mine will be done in a couple of minutes. It's my light stuff and I've got it on the short cycle."

She nodded and headed for the two end machines without saying anything to me or even looking at me. Her face was bent down over her laundry basket. Her long pale hair fell in a straight curtain on either side of her face.

"Actually, this time of day is pretty good for using the laundry because everybody's in class," I said.

She opened a machine and started dumping her stuff into it.

"I should be in class, too, but I was late, so I figured I might as well use the time getting my stuff washed," I said.

She brushed her hand across her face. I couldn't see her face, but I could see her hand. Also, she made a soft gulping sound.

I never waste time being diplomatic when somebody's crying. "What's wrong?" I asked.

She shook her head.

"Flunking something?"

She muttered, "No."

"Then it's got to be a guy," I said.

She turned to look up at me. For sure she was crying. Tears streaked down her face. Her skin was all puffy and red. "How did you know?" she mumbled.

"Who'd know better than me?" I said. "I could fill one of these washing machines with the tears I've shed over guys. Sometime when you've got a week or two to do nothing but listen, I'll tell you about my rotten boyfriend."

She smiled a little at that, but it's rough smiling when you're crying and I said so, adding, "None of them are worth it."

"I know that now," she said. "It's too late."

"Too late for what?" I asked. She could always tell me it wasn't my business and she wouldn't hurt my feelings at all, but she looked to me like she wanted to talk.

She did. She started in slowly, in a mumble. Then her voice rose and she spoke faster and faster. "You know Mark, the guy I go with, or anyway, the guy I thought I went with? Umm, sure, everybody knows Mark, every girl—oh, I don't mean you—and anyway, it's not that so much, it's that he knows every girl, and he keeps saying he loves me, he tells me that, and then I see him with someone else and he says it's nothing, she's just some friend in one of his classes, and I keep believing him, and then last night he broke a date and when my roommate came in, she told me she'd seen him sitting in a back booth at the Den making out with some girl and so I phoned him this morning and asked how his studying was going—because that's what he told me he had to do last night, study—and he said he'd been at the library all night and he'd have to study again tonight and so I slammed down the phone and I hate him!"

"I know what you mean," I said.

The Den is the local off-campus hangout, a dimly lit, smoky place with high-backed booths. On weekends it's a mob scene, fun sometimes, with everyone singing along with the recorded music, but on slow nights it can be half-empty and a lot of couples use the booths to get privacy. It's not too easy finding privacy on campus. Still, the Den isn't that private, either, because even if only a half dozen other people wander through, they're bound to be from the U. and at least one of them is going to be somebody who recognizes you. And reports you to your steady.

Allison shrugged, as though she'd run out of words. And hope.

I said, "Same thing happened to me when I first started dating Rick. Somebody told me she'd seen him with someone else. I wanted to kill him. Or myself."

"What'd you do?" she asked.

"Told him what I thought of him. Had a big fight. Broke up. That was about a thousand fights ago."

"You kept going with him?"

"I love to suffer," I said. "Tell you what I did do, though, if you want to hear."

"Go ahead," she said. Misery really does love company.

"I made up my mind that I wasn't going to be his doormat. I told him that I'd go out with him but not steady, that there were other guys I liked."

"What did he say to that?"

"You wouldn't want me to repeat his language. Oh, he was mad, and we didn't speak for a while, and then we'd go out again, and it kind of went on like that, and we're still dating."

"Do you date other guys?"

"Not exactly," I admitted, "but sort of."

"What's that mean?"

"Okay, let me tell you," I said. "What I do is this. I make friends with lots of guys, guys I meet in classes and stuff, and I go for coffee with them or study with them in the library, or meet them in the cafeteria for meals, see, but if they ask me out, I tell them I'm going with somebody. But I keep them as friends. That's the important thing. That way, Rick sees me with other guys."

"Doesn't he get mad?"

"Sure, but he can't admit it. He can't get mad about me having friends."

"What's the point?" she asked. By now she'd stopped crying.

"Allison, the point is that he knows I know lots of guys, and that I could date them if I wanted to, and that if he dates somebody else, he can be sure that I will, too."

"So you never have dated anyone else, after all?"

"A few times," I said. "When we broke up and he went out with someone else. I dated Jon Austin, who is one of my very best friends. But I don't date him now that Rick and I are back together."

She shrugged and said, "I don't think that would work for me."

"Why not?"

"I don't know any other guys," she said.

"Everybody knows other guys!" I said.

"Not any who'd ask me out," she said.

"Look," I said, "all you've got to do is be seen with them. Mark'll hear about it, believe me. Now what you do is this. Today, when you go over to lunch at the cafeteria, look around until you spot some guy who's in one of your classes and then go sit next to him and ask him something about the class, anything, just be seen talking to him, and when he leaves, get up and walk out with him, and when you get outside, walk a few feet away from him and then turn and wave at him and shout, *see you,* anything.

He doesn't even have to hear. But somebody will see you and Mark will hear."

She got a sort of half smile on her face, which was a big improvement on the way she had been looking.

I said, "Do the same thing in the coffee shop this afternoon, and again tonight at supper, and this evening in the library. You don't even have to know the guy. Pick a different one each time. You can be asking them anything, if they know where the registrar's office is, if they know how to sign up for the computer room, anything! But you'll be seen talking to lots of different guys and trust me, Mark will hear about it."

My first washing machine came to a loud, vibrating stop. While I sorted the wash out of it, putting some of the stuff in the dryer and my better shirts on hangers to drip-dry, Allison sorted her wash. Then my second machine stopped and by the time I'd unloaded it, the third stopped, and by the time I'd moved all that stuff to the dryer, my first dryer was ready to unload.

I carried my drip-dries up to my room on their hangers and put them around the room, hooking the hangers over the curtain rods and closet doors and towel racks. Then I went back and folded sheets and jeans and other stuff into my laundry bag. As I was dragging the heavy bag out of the laundry room, Allison said, "See you, Greta."

I said, "Good luck."

Then I went bump-bump up the stairs, dragging my laundry bag two flights, and made it down the hall to my room just in time to grab the receiver off my wall phone on the third ring.

"Greta?"

My heart did this skip-a-beat thing it always does when I hear his voice. Rick has the lowest, sexiest voice of any guy I've heard.

He said, "I've got a car this afternoon. Let's go to Azuza's and get some real food."

Azuza's was a restaurant a couple of miles from campus where they didn't have a captive clientele and had to serve decent food. They did a steak sandwich that Rick really liked.

"I have a class at two," I said.

"So cut it for once," he said.

The way my day was going, I was never going to get that chapter read before two, anyway. And as I'd already missed two classes, why not miss the third and call the whole day off? Besides, I knew he was asking me to Azuza's as an apology for not taking me to the movie, which meant he really did have to use the computer room.

We owed each other apologies. I shouldn't have blown up at him for canceling, and he shouldn't have pretended that we'd never had a date. As Rick and I had never been much good at giving each other straight-out explanations or apologies, I accepted his offer as my way of saying everything was okay between us.

"I'd love to," I said.

"Pick you up in front of your dorm in twenty minutes and don't be late," he said.

"Make it thirty," I said.

We both knew that no way could I freshen my makeup and steam-curl the ends of my hair that had gone limp and redo the nail polish I'd chipped in twenty minutes. And sometimes Rick was mean about waiting. But I knew that if I didn't look perfect, he wouldn't be attracted to me, so it was better to keep him waiting than to go out with him looking like a mess.

This time he said, "Okay, thirty minutes," and laughed. He really *was* in a good mood.

I was on the curb in thirty minutes flat, having tossed myself back together, though after a morning of rushing to missed classes, falling over guys in paths and hauling laundry up from the basement, I'd have preferred a couple of hours. I required at least that much time to put myself in peak condition appearancewise.

Rick pulled up in somebody's old blue heap and I jumped in.

"Whose wheels?" I asked.

"Guy in my dorm," he said. Rick was never one for long explanations.

I slid down in my seat until I could rest my head on the back and turn my face to watch him. Just looking at his profile practically knocked me out. Movie stars go to plastic surgeons to get profiles like that.

So that he wouldn't think that I had nothing better to do with my life than stare at his profile, I said, "Today's been a total washout. Haven't made it to a single class. If I were in high school, they'd be sending the truant officer after me."

Rick said, "You ever seen a truant officer?"

"On TV," I said. "On a morning kiddie show. The truant officer was always collaring the naughty clown."

"Was that yesterday's episode?" he asked, straight-faced.

I snapped my finger at him, flicking his shoulder, for implying that I still watched clown shows, and said, "Wonder whatever happened to old Oggie Clown? He was the naughty one, and don't give me any lip about the word *naughty*. That's what they called him, Oggie, the Naughty Clown."

"Probably still in the lockup for cutting school," he said.

Rick parked in the lot. I followed him into Azuza's, a low building of brick and wide, glare-tinted windows, with an overhang of shake roof. Inside the waitress led us to a window booth with a view of the parking lot and the highway.

The booths were done in imitation brown leather. Above the tables hung Old West–style brass lanterns. Wagon wheels mounted on low walls divided the space into small dining areas. The inner walls, away from the windows, were covered with sepia-tinted photo murals of cowboys and herds of cattle.

"Ah, the real world," I sighed as I picked up my menu. I loved the U., with its ivy and Gothic, and everyone either students and wearing jeans or faculty and wearing tweed, but sometimes it was nice to get away and see different things.

"Real food," Rick said.

After we'd ordered, he said, "How come you missed your morning classes?"

As I wasn't about to satisfy his ego by telling him I'd been too upset by him to go to my nine o'clock, I said, "I went back to the dorm after breakfast and got to talking to Marci, and next thing I knew, it was already nine-fifteen. And then I started out in time to get to my eleven o'clock, but—and you are not going to believe this—I fell over some guy."

He didn't say anything, just sat there looking at me, waiting for me to go on.

"I did. I was running down the back path to cut across that footbridge by the lower field, and this guy was all crouched down in the grass."

Rick raised his eyebrows. That pleased me. I didn't usually get that much reaction out of him.

I said, "And I ran right into him, hit him with my foot, you know, and kind of did a flip up and across him and knocked us both flat."

"What was he doing in the grass?" Rick asked.

"Looking for fiddleheads. He had this notebook and he was keeping a record of how fast they grew. For some science class, botany, that's what he said. Only he was wearing this shirt that was kind of grass-colored so he blended right in and I never saw him until I'd practically killed us both, so by the time I got up and asked him what he was doing, and checked to be sure we were both alive, well, it was too late to make it to tennis."

"So then what'd you do?"

"Went back to the dorm and spent an exciting two hours in the laundry room listening to the soapsuds slosh. It's really been a thrilling day. You can see why I was so eager to get away this afternoon."

"And here I thought it was the sandwiches," Rick said, and gave me one of his long, gorgeous, dark-eyed looks.

We both knew perfectly well why I'd accepted his invitation, that it was to be with him. Not that I'd say so. It's no good letting boys know how much you care about them, especially boys like Rick who automatically expect total devotion.

I said, "That, too. I wouldn't have cut lit for anything less than Azuza's."

When the waitress brought our steak sandwiches and shakes, we quieted down to eat. Or at least, Rick did. He goes at his food in that steady way boys do, as though they're refueling. I pick around the edges more, and stop to look around. Azuza's wasn't too busy, as we were past the lunch hour, but there was a family in another booth, a mother and father and a couple of little kids, too small for school, who acted tired, rubbing their eyes. I guessed maybe they were on a trip. And there were three women in another booth, all wearing suits but kind of frilly blouses and lots of jewelry, I couldn't decide if they were working women or shoppers. I related all this to Rick, who ate away, glancing up at me occasionally.

I did get his attention when a Mercedes pulled into the lot and I described it as well as the two guys who climbed out of it. Rick looked out the window at the car. I looked at the guys. They were in three-piece suits.

"You think they're bankers?" I asked.

"This year's model," he said, impressed by the car. "What'd one of those cost, I wonder?"

We finished eating and headed back to the U. Rick said, "Where you want me to drop you?"

"Any place," I said. "I'll probably stop by my room and get my notebook and then I'd better get over to the library to do some studying."

Rick parked in the lot for student cars, near his dorm, saying he'd leave the car there for his friend. There wasn't anyone in the lot except us and a lot of empty cars. Rick slid his arms around me and pulled me into one of his wonderful, warm kisses.

"I've missed you," he whispered. He'd seen me at breakfast, but I knew what he meant. Whenever we fought, I missed him terribly.

We walked back across the street, up a path, and stopped at the main walk that ran the length of the campus. We hadn't said much, but we had our arms linked around each other's waists, and just being together like that was like talking for hours.

It wasn't until we moved away from each other to head off in our separate directions that Rick said, "Watch where you're going now. Don't trip over any more muggers."

I laughed and said, "David isn't a mugger."

Rick said, "David?"

Right away I knew I shouldn't have let on that I knew David's name, because that way Rick knew that I had stopped to talk to him for a while. People don't exchange names when they bump, say excuse me, and immediately part company.

But I wasn't going to make any explanations. All I said was, "Yeah, David."

"David who?"

I shrugged, trying to look nonchalant. "I dunno. Just David."

"You didn't tell me you knew him," Rick said.

"Didn't I?" I said. I thought about saying that when you've knocked a guy over and sprawled all over him, you're no longer strangers, but I decided that would irritate Rick more. Instead I said, "I don't really, just his name. If you get done in the computer room, why don't you call me?"

"Okay," he said, so I thought everything was still fine between us.

3

But it wasn't. Rick didn't phone that night or the next day. When I rang his room, nobody answered. I looked for him at mealtimes in the cafeteria. He wasn't there. And I didn't see him anywhere on campus.

Three days later he still hadn't called. I was back to moping about and standing in hot showers.

Actually, standing in the dorm shower was sometimes very close to going to a psychiatrist, not that I'd ever been to a real one. But it was like going to the ones on TV, where you stretch out on a couch and tell them all your troubles.

I was rubbing shampoo in my hair, trying not to get it in my eyes, with hot water streaming down over me, when someone shouted, "That you, Greta?"

"Yeah," I shouted back over the noise of the water. "Who's that?"

"Inger," she said.

I rubbed the water out of my eyes and peered around the edge of the shower curtain.

Inger Peters stood across the room by the row of sinks, her foot propped up on the edge of one sink. She was thin and long-legged and she looked like she was doing some sort of aerobics, standing on one leg that way.

"What're you doing?" I asked.

"Shaving my legs," she said, glancing at me. She had a thin face and long-lashed eyes, and her black hair was cut about an inch long all over her head. On anyone else it might have looked terrible, but on Inger it looked terrific.

I ducked back under the water and closed the curtain.

"Do you still date Rick?" she called.

"Sometimes more than other times," I called back.

"Sounds like me and Hal. One day he's talking about getting married and the next day he's talking about hitchhiking around the world with some other guys."

"One day Rick says he'll phone, and the next three days I don't hear a word from him," I said.

"Guys are weird," Inger agreed.

I said, "It's not as though I told him I owned him. I try not to push. I give him lots of space. So wouldn't you think he'd keep in touch, even if he only has time to tell me he's busy?"

"Hal said he'd come to my town to meet my folks over Christmas, so I phoned home and arranged it with them and everything, and then the day before winter break, he breezes in, cheery as you please, and says he's heading for a ski lodge and won't see me till January."

I turned off the shower and stepped out, wrapped in my towel.

As I rubbed my wet hair with my other towel, I said, "You know what their trouble is? Guys want to own girls. They want to feel a girl is all theirs. But they don't want to *be* owned."

Inger said, "That sounds very one-sided and unfair."

"It is," I said. "We shouldn't put up with it."

"What else can we do?" she asked.

"Be as independent as they are," I said. "Make other plans, be busy when they call, let them know we have our own lives and that we are not hanging around breathlessly waiting for them."

She said, "If I did that, Hal would probably quit calling."

I put on my robe and collected my shampoo, conditioners, sponge, brush, soap, towels, face cloth, shampoo brush and the rest of my stuff, and headed out the door. "At least I feel better, knowing someone else has the same problems."

"Me, too," she said.

As I reached for the door handle, my roommate, Marci, pushed it open from the hallway.

She said, "Greta, Rick's on the phone."

"Remember to let him know you have your own life," Inger shouted after me as I raced down the hall to my room.

When I was inside, I stopped by the wall phone, its receiver dangling on its cord, and took a couple of deep breaths. I didn't want to sound as though I'd been running. Then in my calmest voice, I said, "Hello?"

"Where were you?" he said.

"Down the hall. Did you get your paper finished?"

"Paper?" he said.

"The one you were working on in the computer room."

"Oh that! Yeah, it's okay. It's done. But listen, honey, I've got a lot bigger problem and you're the only person who can help me with it."

Whatever it was, I hoped he didn't need it in the next ten minutes, as I needed at least forty minutes to put myself together.

"Honey," he said, a second time. He almost never called me honey. "I've broken the antenna on my TV, and I've got to watch a documentary tonight for notes for my anthro class, and then I've got to have a book that they don't have at the U. But I called the public library and they're holding it for me, and there's a radio shop where you can get the antenna about a block from the library."

"Me?"

"Greta, I've got a seminar this afternoon so I can't go, and I've got to have the antenna and the book and even then, I'll be up all night doing the darn report and if it isn't turned in at nine o'clock tomorrow, I'm dead in anthro."

I said, "Gee, I'd like to help, but I've got a lit class at two."

"If I flunk anthro, I'm washed out! You can miss a lit class, nobody'll notice, but if I cut seminar, there's only eight people in it, so there's no way the prof won't notice and he's been looking for an excuse to drop a bomb on me."

"But, Rick," I said.

He shouted, "Okay, if you don't care, forget it."

"Of course I care," I said, trying to sound really caring. Right after that I was going to explain that I'd be glad to get his antenna and book, under any other circumstances, but as I'd already missed lit the day we went to Azuza's, and that was only three days ago, I couldn't miss it again.

But before I could launch into any of that, he said in this really sweet voice that makes me feel like my insides are hot fudge, "Honey, you're the only person I can depend on. You're a doll. Now grab a paper and I'll give you the address of the radio store and the model number on the antenna and the title of the book."

So I wrote it all down. He told me again how wonderful I was. I felt important and wonderful.

After I hung up, I remembered Inger repeating my own advice to let him know that I had my own life. For sure I knew all the right ways to handle boys and for sure I'd never been able to use any of them with Rick.

And I'd had my day so well organized, too. I'd made it to my morning classes, gone to lunch hoping to run into Rick in the cafeteria and treat him to a casual but friendly greeting, nothing eager. When he wasn't there, I'd consoled myself that that was just as well as my hair was limp from tennis. So I'd gulped lunch and dashed back to shower, which would both drown my disappointment and give me a chance to do my hair, planning that after my two o'clock I could circle through the usual places he was most apt to be, confident of my looks if of nothing else.

Instead, there I was at two-thirty standing on the bus corner waiting for the unreliable city bus to show up. I'd thought about waiting until after lit class.

Then I'd checked the bus schedule. There was a bus at quarter to three and nothing more until four o'clock. It took twenty minutes to get uptown. From there it was twelve blocks out to the library which I could either walk or wait for another bus, and Rick thought the library closed at five, so what else could I do?

I stood on one foot and then the other, peering down the street in the direction from which the bus would come. Maybe it should have cheered me that the sky had cleared to a brilliant blue, and that clusters of daffodils shone like sunlight in the shrubbery beds that lined the campus walkways, but it didn't. The best I could hope for was that my lit prof would be so busy gazing out the window, she wouldn't say anything important in her lecture.

A car pulled up to the curb and Jon leaned across the seat from the driver's side to peer out the open window at me. "Greta? Need a ride?"

I crossed my arms on the windowsill and leaned down to say, "I have to go all the way uptown to the main library and then to a store."

"Hop in, I'll drive you."

"I have a couple of errands. It could take a while."

"I'm free," he said, and smiled.

"You're not free, you're priceless," I said and got into the car. "What's that saying? A pearl beyond price?"

"Tell me more," he said, still grinning, as he drove me toward town.

I said, "Wouldn't want to destroy your modesty. It's half your charm."

"What's the other half?" he asked.

I laughed and gave him a sideways glance through my eyelashes. He expected me to tease him, so I did.

"If I told you that, you wouldn't be modest anymore."

His large hands moved on the wheel, tapping out a rhythm. I watched the scenery slide by, from campus greenery to neighborhoods of neat houses with carefully tended gardens, to apartment rows, and finally to a confusion of storefronts and billboards.

"I don't know how close to the library I can park," he said.

"Drop me off and circle the block. All I've got to do is run in and grab a book."

"Won't you need to look it up and get a call number?"

"Rick's got it on hold at the desk," I said, and then could have bitten my tongue.

"You're picking up a book for Rick?" he asked.

"He has a seminar this afternoon and he needs this book to finish a report for his anthro class and it's due tomorrow."

Jon didn't say more, just dropped me at the library, circled the block and was there waiting when I came running back down the steps with the book in my hand.

The radio store was in a small shopping center with a parking lot. Jon parked and came into the store with me. I found a clerk who found the antenna model that I needed, paid for it and headed back out, and Jon still didn't say anything, but before we got in the car, he said, "Want to stop for coffee?"

I really wanted to go back to campus and take Rick his stuff. Even if he had to spend the evening studying, we could still go to supper together. But Jon had been so kind to drive me to town, and it was only quarter to four, so it seemed the least I could do.

I gave him a big smile and said, "I'd love that, but let me treat you because you've been such a life-saver."

There was a coffee shop in the mall, one of those small places with metal chairs and tables done in curled iron and painted white. The table top was glass. The chairs were almost too small to hold anyone the size of Jon. The waitress looked motherly and bored. Her tired expression didn't match her flowered dress and the ruffled white apron and headband.

After she'd served us coffee and croissants and then gone back to her own cup of coffee at a table on the far side of the otherwise empty shop, Jon said, "What happened to your two o'clock?"

It was sweet of him to remember my schedule. Rick never did. "They weren't doing anything important," I said.

"Not as important as running errands for Rick," he said.

"He's really afraid he'll flunk that class," I said.

The muscles in his face tightened beneath his freckled skin. He gave me one of his searching stares that always left me feeling that he could see right through to my brain.

He said, "Greta, a guy is supposed to take care of his girl, not the other way around. He shouldn't be sending you off alone on a city bus to run his errands."

Now that business of a guy taking care of his girl is one I adore. I have this poster over my bed in my dorm room. It shows this gorgeous, musclebound hunk of a guy standing between a dragon-type monster and a beautiful damsel. In one upraised hand he's brandishing a sword. His other powerful arm is held out in front of the girl to protect her. You know, looking at the picture, that the only way that monster will reach that girl is by killing the hunk first. Talk about excitement, romance, drama!

Great stuff for posters, but real life isn't like that. Sometimes I wish it were, sure, and then I remind myself that those dragon-plagued princesses didn't have hair dryers. Or cars. Or TV.

I said, "Jon, I am eighteen, old enough to ride a bus alone."

"Old enough to think for yourself, too. So why do you let Rick tell you what to do?"

I tried to match his stare with what I hoped was a sincere gaze. "Jon, it's a gorgeous day, lit class is a bore and I wanted an excuse to cut."

"You cut to run Rick's errands."

Why is it that guys always tell you to think for yourself and then turn around and criticize your decisions? As I didn't want to argue with Jon, I tried to think of something clever to say to change the subject. A magazine article that I'd once read said that when a conversation with a guy turned tense, toss him a compliment.

I gave it my best shot, eyes wide, smile bright. I said, "I'm glad I did cut because now I'm here with you."

Whoever wrote that article must have known Jon. He grinned and stopped lecturing me.

Jon was so much easier to figure out than Rick. For sure he was easier to get along with. That's because he was the right type of guy.

Guys come in types, and it's good to know how to

tell them apart. My roommate, Marci, has a younger cousin, Joanne, who is still in high school, and as Jon sat there smiling at me, I remembered the first time I'd met Joanne and she'd asked me something about boys. Right away I could see she needed advice, so I'd told her what I knew.

"Joanne," I'd said, "boys come in three types: jocks, hunks and your average guy." I'd told her then to avoid the jocks; they were too tied up with sports. And the gorgeous hunks always wanted to have their own way. "Concentrate on the guy who is average cute and dresses right because he wants you to like him. He'll be sweet and dependable."

That was Jon, sweet and dependable.

And Rick was a gorgeous hunk.

After Joanne had met both of them, she'd once said to me, "Why don't you follow your own advice? If you had good sense, you'd drop Rick and grab Jon."

Certainly she was right. Looking at Jon, with his kind smile and his pleasant good looks, trying so hard to impress me with his thoughtfulness, I knew how much he cared about me.

If I'd had any sense, I'd have forgotten Rick and fallen for Jon, then and there. But what does good sense have to do with love?

That's another thing I know about boys. It's hard to think about them and keep one's thoughts perfectly sensible.

That evening I met Rick in the cafeteria for supper and gave him his book and TV antenna. He was wearing a white turtleneck pullover that set off his dark coloring.

He glanced at the book and said, "This had better have the information I need, or I'm dead."

I knew he was worried about his anthropology paper, but still, he could have said thank you. I said, "I cut a class to get that for you."

He gave me one of his dark gazes, saying, "You're a doll."

When he looked at me like that, cutting a two o'clock seemed like no bother at all.

But the next day when I sat in class and watched the prof pass a quiz back to the other students, I had other thoughts. To the girl at the next desk, I whispered, "I didn't know we were having a quiz."

She whispered back, "It was announced three days ago."

With this awful hollow feeling building up in my midsection, I realized that the quiz must have been announced on the day I'd cut to go to Azuza's with Rick.

Why hadn't I thought to ask someone in the class if we'd had any assignments? That had been stupid of me. Not knowing what to do, I stopped by the professor's desk after class.

My heart started beating in my throat, which was really dumb but I couldn't make it stop, I was that nervous. My voice came out all ragged. "Excuse me, I think I missed a quiz yesterday."

"Yes," she said, not looking up at me.

"Is there—is there any way I can make it up?"

"If you have a form from the health office that you were ill."

"No," I mumbled.

She looked up, met my gaze and smiled. "It wasn't an important quiz. It was only twenty percent of this week's grade; the rest is the paper, so it shouldn't hurt you too much."

There was no answer at all that I could make to

that, as I didn't know anything about a paper. I nodded my thanks, then turned and dashed out of the room and down the corridor and out of the building. Halfway across the lawn, disappearing down a path, was the girl who sat next to me in class. Since I didn't know anyone else in that class, I went flying after her.

By the time I caught up with her, I was panting for breath. "Wait," I gasped.

"What's wrong?" She stopped to stare at me. So did half a dozen other students who were wandering by. I must have had a really wild look on my face.

"Tell me about the paper! When did she assign a paper?"

"In lit?" Her eyes widened. "Didn't you do that, either? Oh gosh, she assigned it the same day she told us about the quiz. It's due tomorrow."

"Tomorrow! What's the subject?"

"You're to pick any of the authors we've covered so far and take any four of their works and compare them."

"Compare four authors?" I said.

"No, compare four works of one author, four works that we haven't covered in class. Oh, and the works are supposed to be stories or essays, not poems, and the paper should be about ten pages long."

"Ten pages!"

"I've been working on mine all week," she said, and gave me this very doubtful look.

If she felt doubtful, it was nothing compared to how I felt. In a blind panic, I took off for the library, sure I could never get four works read, much less write ten pages comparing them, before our next class. And if I turned the paper in late, I might as well not turn it in at all, because by the time the prof deducted points for being late, and twenty percent off for missing the quiz, I'd have a zero for the week. As it was, I was carrying a very weak C in lit. I felt a solid D coming on.

By a stroke of luck I found a library assistant who had taken the same lit class the previous semester and was familiar with the course. He knew right where to find a good collected-works edition of one of the authors and he also stood over me and gave me some good suggestions, as I wrote rapidly in my notebook.

"Compare his use of subplots, because this guy is especially noted for his subplots, and be sure to use the third story in the book, because it's his most famous, and then I'd suggest you use the seventh one, also, because it's one of his least quoted and gives the impression you're really well read," he said, and rattled off a string of other points to include.

By the time I left the library, my hand ached from writing, and it wasn't until I was running up the steps in my dorm that I even stopped to think about that library assistant. He'd been cute, I was sure of that, but what had he actually looked like?

I couldn't even remember, that's how upset I was about that paper.

As I dashed into my room, my roommate, Marci, was taking the phone off the hook and saying, "Hello?"

I threw myself across my bed and opened my book to the third story. Leafing through it, I saw that it was over twenty pages long. Worse, as I checked through the rest of the book, I saw that none of the stories was much shorter.

Marci said, "Phone for you, Greta."

"I can't talk to anybody," I shouted, still in shock. How was I ever going to get all those pages read, plus figure out comparisons and write a ten-page paper?

The print swam in front of my eyes. I reread the first paragraph of the story three times without understanding a word. Taking a deep breath, I willed myself to calm down.

It was then that I realized what Marci had said.

Turning over on the bed, I said. "Who was on the phone?"

By that time Marci had returned to her desk, where she was busy typing. She said, "Somebody named David."

"Okay," I said, and went back to my reading. As long as it wasn't Rick, I didn't care who it was, because I didn't have time to talk to anyone else.

4

It was a nightmare night. Marci, who has to be the best roommate in the world, did her best, answering the phone, talking in low whispers and tiptoeing around me while I read through eighty pages of short stories. My eyes felt like those cartoon characters' eyes, the kind that spin like pinwheels.

I heard Marci whispering into the phone, "I'll ask her tomorrow, Joanne. She's tied up now."

For a moment I wondered what Joanne, who is Marci's cousin, wanted, and I almost turned and asked, but then I thought about flunking and getting kicked out of college, and I riveted my eyes back on that book.

Later I heard her whispering, "I know, Steve, but I think she's flunking something." Steve is Marci's steady.

And once there was a tap on the door and Marci

answered and slipped outside into the hall. Somebody wailed, "But I've got to ask her," and then again I heard Marci's whisper, though I couldn't catch the words. She came back in the room and closed the door softly.

By the time I'd finished the reading and jotted down lists of comparisons, it was midnight and Marci was getting ready for bed.

I knew that if I stayed in the room, typing, she'd cover her head with her pillow and not complain, but I also knew she wouldn't get much sleep. So I packed up my portable typewriter and headed for the door.

Marci said, "Is there anything I can do to help you?"

"No," I said. "It isn't hard and I understand it, it's just an assignment that takes time, like four days, and it's my own stupid fault I didn't know about it four days ago."

"Well, okay," she said, "but if you need pages retyped or anything, come on back and wake me up."

I gave her a weak grin, which was the best I could manage, and trudged down the hall to the swinging door that led onto the balcony. The balcony is a narrow, carpeted strip edged by an old wooden balustrade, that runs the width of the lounge below. The lounge is a large room, two stories high, filled with couches and overstuffed chairs. Occasionally it's used for dorm parties. More often, it serves as an all-night study hall for people whose roommates are sleeping. Also, as it is entered from the first floor, it is occasionally used by couples who want to sit around and talk after a date.

Anyone coming up the walk looks into the

lounge's high windows, and anyone on the balcony looks down on it, so it isn't private enough for anything more than conversation.

That night its sole occupant was a girl curled in a chair, her head bent over a book.

The total furnishings of the balcony are one wooden typing table and one straight-backed chair. I spread out my typewriter, book and paper, and got right to work.

An hour or so later I glanced down through the balustrade and saw that the other girl had given up and left. I typed on.

An hour after that I stood up to stretch. My back and neck felt as though I'd spent the last six hours lifting weights, they were that stiff. Taking a three-minute break, I returned to the hallway, dropped my coins into the soft drink machine, and chose a caffeine-loaded drink. After setting the opened can on the floor next to the typing table, I got right back to typing.

Several times during the night, when I'd reached for the soda or go back to the machine for another, I'd glance at the tall windows of the lounge below me. The lounge was almost dark, with only two heavily shaded lamps left on all night. Outside the dark windows, dark maples swayed above the walk, their branches lit on the undersides by the walkway lamps.

And then the next time I looked up, the lamps had gone out and the sky was pale gray.

By the time I finished the last page, checked it over and packed up my stuff, sunlight made a wide strip across the room from its eastern angle, zigzagging up and down over the couches, then shooting straight across the carpet to the next row of furniture. Outside, people were hurrying by on the walk to head for the cafeteria for breakfast.

I stumbled into my room just as Marci was rushing out. "Did you get it done?" she asked.

"Barely," I said. "It's probably terrible, but at least it's done."

She gave me a long, worried look and said, "Greta, why don't you go throw yourself in the shower and I'll proofread this for you?"

Like I said, she was the nicest roommate in the world. I was too zonked to turn down such a fantastic offer.

When I returned from my shower, feeling a few degrees closer to being a human being again, my papers were neatly stacked by my typewriter. Glancing at them, I saw that Marci had corrected typos and spelling errors and even done a complete retype of the last page. I pulled my wadded-up copy from the wastebasket and saw why. I'd made so many errors, no one but Marci could have figured it out.

In case I didn't see her later in the day, I drew a big heart on a piece of paper, wrote 'A million thanks!' in the center, and left it on her desk.

By the time I'd dressed and dried my hair and all that, I'd missed breakfast and barely made it to my nine o'clock. After sitting through that class, holding my eyes open with my fingertips, I made a straight line for the cafeteria, grabbed coffee and a doughnut and, after gulping it down, headed for lower campus. If there was one thing I didn't feel like, it was tennis, but this wasn't the day to cut another class. I mean, even though they don't pull pop quizzes in gym class, it's the one place where they positively do take attendance and count it into the grade.

Ever try to play tennis in your sleep? Don't. It's

murder. I hit the showers again, this time the gym shower, hoping it would keep me going until two. Then I dashed back to my dorm to get my lit paper, gave it one last glance-over, realized I'd attributed a quote to the wrong story—a point Marci couldn't catch as she hadn't read the stories—and, letting out a shriek that should have awakened anyone who might still be sleeping, I flung myself into my desk chair to retype the third page.

Then I remembered that the book I'd used was on reserve and had to be returned by noon, which was already past, but if I looked desperate enough maybe the librarian wouldn't cancel my library-use privileges, which they could do for four days for late returns on reserve books. So by the time I'd taken care of all that, and yes, I did look desperate enough, and run from my dorm to the library to my two o'clock, I'd missed lunch but I had that wretched paper in on time.

I think the prof gave a lecture, in fact, I am sure she did, but afterwards, I couldn't remember a word. All I could remember was turning in the paper and then sitting stiffly upright, battling exhaustion, terrified that I would fall asleep and land on the floor. I didn't think that if I did that, she'd be impressed, at least, not impressed the way I wanted her to be.

At three I headed back toward the Union building, thinking I'd get something to eat in the coffee shop and then go back to my room to sleep. But when I reached the lower path, I was shaking so hard I was honestly afraid I'd fall.

It was a case of delayed panic. My brain wouldn't work. Even my vision seemed blurred. All I could see was the bridge and the little woods that edged the stream and a patch of very green spring grass shining under a very bright afternoon sun.

I crossed the bridge and sank down on the grass. I thought maybe if I sat in the sun for a minute I'd feel better. Until that moment, I hadn't noticed how warm the day was, how much more like summer than spring. Closing my eyes, I slid slowly down and stretched out and rested my head on my arm. Beneath my face, the grass smelled sweet.

I was so tired I didn't even dream, though I did have a jumble of disconnected thoughts. There was Marci, looking worried, and Jon frowning, and Rick scolding, and my lit prof glaring, and a tennis ball headed right at me.

And then someone shook me and said, "You okay?"

I rolled over and found myself staring into those warm brown eyes. David was crouched down beside me, peering at me. For some reason that I couldn't figure, he looked very worried.

"I was sleeping," I mumbled.

"Here? Outside?"

"What's the matter, is this your space, nobody else can trespass?" I was too tired to be polite.

He leaned back and gave me room to sit up. "No, only I thought, uh, sorry I woke you."

It hit me why he looked worried. "Bet you thought I'd tripped over something again and this time knocked myself out."

His nice, square face went all embarrassed around his grin. "Something like that," he admitted.

"I didn't get any sleep at all last night," I explained. "I had this horrendous paper to do."

"You want me to go away and let you get back to sleep?"

Laughing, I stood up. "No, I'm fine now. How are your fiddleheads growing?"

"That's what I came to check," he said. "Come on along and look. There should be skunk cabbages further up the stream."

Who could resist an invitation to visit a skunk cabbage? Maybe I'm no scientist, but I can ooh and ah over new foliage as well as anyone. I tagged along.

David held out his hand to help me down the stream's bank. His hand was like the rest of him, firm and warm. We wandered at the water's edge, picking our way through the marshes, beneath a lacy canopy of willows with their new leaves unfolding, until the water's turning path took us out of sight of the bridge.

"Think I'll wade," he said, pulling off his shoes.

"Good idea," I said, and stood on one foot to untie the laces on my sneaker. When I leaned dangerously to one side, David put his arm around my shoulders to keep me from falling. The boy obviously had a fixation about my proclivity to collapse.

When I was barefoot, and solidly standing on both feet, he moved away from me, walking in front of me into the water. It was shallow and sun warmed. The stream's bed was mossy. With each step, mud oozed around my feet.

"I haven't waded in mud since I was six years old," I said, laughing.

"Nice, huh? Hey, here's skunk cabbages!"

Yes, they are pretty, with their wide yellow petals, and no, they do not smell pretty. However, the spring air was so filled with sunlight on blossoming trees and meadow flowers that the skunk cabbages couldn't compete.

David pulled a small notebook from his hip pocket and did a sketch. With only a few lines, he caught the graceful newness of the plants.

"You're awfully good at that," I said.

"Think so?" He gave me a pleased smile.

We found patches of sweet woodruff, their tight white buds promising to open at any moment, and marsh flowers in shades of pale green and yellow that neither of us could identify, and even an early violet and a wild narcissus.

We also spotted tadpoles and thrushes. Small creatures rustled through the grassy banks, keeping out of sight. And an occasional brightly colored insect hovered above the water. David watched everything, catching shadowy shapes with his pencil. He gave them personality, made each leaf and creature more interesting than I'd at first thought it could be. Watching him sketch, I forgot all about being tired.

Instead, I found myself noticing details, light reflections, odd angles of branches, the way a bird cocked its head, that sort of thing.

When David finished a sketch and glanced at me to see if I was still there, I couldn't help noticing that there were gold flecks in his light brown eyes.

It's the sort of thing writers always give characters in romance books, but David was the first person I'd ever met who actually had gold flecks in his eyes. I decided that maybe it was only a trick of the sunlight. I was surrounded by gold flecks, glittering off the water and the marsh grass and the whispering trees.

We climbed up the bank to a dry patch of grass. While David wrote notes in the margins around his sketches, identifying plant parts with words like *stamen, pistil* and so forth, I braided dandelion stems into a bracelet.

When he noticed what I was doing, he laughed. "Another leftover skill from your six-year-old mud-wading days?"

"I have a very narrow range of talents."

"Okay, I'll be honest with you. You've got a talent I've always envied."

"What? Weaving dandelions?"

"Yes," he said. "I could never do that. They always break for me."

I said generously, "Make you a deal. I'll trade you this bracelet for one of your sketches."

He handed me the notebook. "Take them all."

"What, and be responsible for you flunking botany?" I said. "No, fair's fair, and this bracelet is worth one sketch."

After I'd pulled out the page with the sketch of the skunk cabbage on it, I handed him the bracelet. He slipped it over his hand and held out his wrist to admire it.

Our eyes met and we both laughed.

And then for some funny reason I had this weird, dizzy feeling. At first I thought, come on, Greta, he's cute, but he's not Rick. But then I realized that I really was dizzy.

"You all right?" he asked, in the same worried tone that he'd asked me earlier, when he'd found me sleeping by the bridge.

"I guess so, only I feel kind of—kind of faint."

David put his hand on my shoulder. "Probably because you didn't get any sleep last night."

"Now don't give me that worried look again," I mumbled, and then I realized I was mumbling. Somehow, my mouth didn't seem to be able to work right. I felt his shoulder against my head and knew that he was holding me to keep me from falling over, and this time I was very glad he was.

David didn't say anything more, just sat there quietly hanging on to me, his arm around me, while I waited for the world to stop spinning. As my head cleared, my stomach began to ache.

I sat up straight and David's arm dropped away from me. "You know what, I think I'm hungry."

"You get faint when you get hungry?"

"I haven't had anything to eat today except a doughnut. I missed breakfast and then I missed lunch."

While I sat there with all the animation of a rag doll, David pulled my socks out of my sneakers, put them on me, then put my sneakers on my feet and tied the laces.

"I really could do that myself," I protested.

"Uh-huh," he said, and caught hold of my hands and pulled me to my feet. We stumbled across the meadow, David's arm around my waist and me feeling very dumb, taking the direct route to the bridge.

"This is stupid," I said. "I felt fine not twenty minutes ago."

He said, "Uh-huh," again, nothing more, and steered me across the bridge, through the woods path and up onto the back patio of the Union building. The patio is a wide concrete strip edged by a low brick wall that overlooks the woods, and it's filled with hundreds of metal deck chairs, the type with arms. I sat down in the first one I reached. I felt considerably more secure sitting in a chair with arms.

"Will you be all right for a few minutes by yourself?" he asked.

"Of course, but where are you going?"

"Be right back," he said, and dashed off.

That's the last of him, I thought, as I closed my eyes and tried to rest. He'd write me off as the campus kook and work hard at never letting our paths cross again.

But I was wrong. While my thoughts were still drifting off in odd directions, he returned.

"Greta?"

I opened my eyes. David stood in front of me, holding a cafeteria tray.

"You feel well enough to eat?" he asked.

"That's what I need, something to eat," I said, and made an effort to give him a big, everything's-okay smile.

David pulled around chairs, putting one between us to serve as a table, and placed the tray on it. He'd gone to the coffee shop rather than the main cafeteria. The tray contained two steak sandwiches and two milkshakes, coffee shop food.

"There's a huge line at the cafeteria now, and I didn't want to wait," he explained, "but you can always go get your regular supper later when you feel better."

"What's supper?" I asked, as I picked up my sandwich.

He gave me a funny look, wrinkling his short, wide nose. "Chicken stew."

"Wow, I think I'll look you up every chicken stew night and do my fainting act," I said. Because students had pass cards to the cafeteria but had to pay for coffee shop food, I added, "Let me pay you back. What do I owe you?"

"Nothing," he said.

"Sure, I do," I said. It wasn't as though he were some guy I was dating. Or even some guy I knew very well.

"No, you don't," he said.

"If you go around buying supper for every faint girl on campus, you won't have any money for tuition," I said. "Come on, what do I owe you?"

I'd had a couple of bites of the sandwich and several swallows of milkshake, and I was feeling much better.

"Make you a deal," he said slowly, watching me. "Next time I feel faint, I'll phone you and you can bring me supper and we'll be even."

"Do you feel faint often?" I asked. "You don't look like the fainting type."

"What does the fainting type look like?"

"Actually, in magazine stories, fainting types are always female, usually eighteenth century. I think it had something to do with tight corset stays. Nowadays, women faint so seldom, most men don't know what to do."

Surprised, he said, "What's that supposed to mean?"

I felt much better, relaxed, expansive, talkative— my old self. I launched into one of my long explanations. "David, read any old historical romance, or watch an old costume movie. There's always a girl who swoons away at some point, and when she does, she sinks slowly and gracefully, giving the hero plenty of time to catch her in his arms and carry her to some handy couch or grassy knoll where he dabs her forehead with a perfumed lace hanky until she comes round with a flutter of eyelashes."

"True," he said.

"But nowadays, women faint so seldom, nobody even remembers what the word *swoon* meant. And if a woman does start to swoon, who'd rush forward? Probably some guy fresh from a first aid class, who'd tell everyone to stand back while he stretches her arms over her head and starts pumping her ribs up and down."

"And she comes to coughing," he laughed.

"Uh-huh. The romance of the lace hanky is a lost art."

"At least I didn't pump your ribs," David said.

"You may be some throwback to historic man," I said.

"Next time I'll let you fall on your face in the stream," he said.

Finishing up my supper, I said, "Seriously, you are an absolute angel and I owe you a supper because you have probably saved my life, but now I have to get back to my room because I still have a couple hours' worth of studying and I'm not even sure I can stay awake that long."

As I began to gather up paper cups and napkins and pile them on the tray to return to the clearing counter, he said, "Let that go, I'll get it."

"Next time the whole works are on me, serving, paying, clearing," I said.

"See you around," he said.

I gave him a wink, which is one of those things I am always doing even though my mother says girls shouldn't wink, and hurried across the patio, down the stairs and along the path to Smith Hall. It wasn't until I was all the way there and upstairs and rushing along the corridor to my room that I remembered that he had phoned me sometime the previous night.

I distinctly remembered Marci saying that David had phoned. I'd been too busy to think about it at the time, but now that I had time, I thought. I didn't know any other David on campus. It had to be that David. But I didn't even know his last name.

And I hadn't told him mine.

How had he known my phone number?

I very nearly U-turned to go back and ask, but then I decided that if I did, he'd figure I was leading him on, interested in him, and of course I was, but only as a friend, because for sure I didn't need another guy complicating my life. So I didn't go back.

But I did still wonder.

5

A few days later, after I'd totally put David out of my mind and stopped wondering why he'd phoned, he popped back into my life.

My relationship with Rick was on again. We'd spent two evenings in a row together, and he'd been reasonably apologetic when I'd told him how I'd missed a test and almost missed an important assignment the day I cut to pick up his book and antenna. I'd met him at three in the coffee shop, and afterwards he walked back to my room with me.

"If Marci's gone, maybe I'll come in and study for a while," he said.

He was climbing the stairs ahead of me. I reached up and jabbed him in the ribs with my finger. "Okay, but you can't smoke."

"Says who?"

"Says me," I said. "The last time you smoked in

our room, Marci could smell the smoke in her closet."

"Did she complain?"

"She didn't cheer," I said. "Anyhow, it's not good for you. Look at all those reports on the terrible diseases people get from smoking."

"Quit nagging," he said.

We turned down the corridor past the open doors into other rooms. Our rooms started out being identical in the fall, each one with a bare linoleum floor, walls painted pale nothing colors, two tall, narrow windows, two cots with striped mattresses, two formica-topped desks with matching chairs in a pale blond wood, a couple of built-in dressers, a long mirror, and two closets. Carefully planned blah.

During the year the rooms underwent a metamorphosis. They grew decorations. The original bare furnishings were like naked trees that had sprouted leaves, hidden beneath their finery. Each room was an individual collection of bright spreads and throw pillows, the linoleum hidden beneath rugs and carpets, the walls papered with posters. Kites and Chinese lanterns and mobiles and wind chimes and a variety of other colorful decorations hung from the ceilings.

I'd packed away the Holly Hobbie spread my first week at school and soon after replaced it with this terrific leopard-spotted sheet. And then I'd covered my half of the walls with my posters and Marci'd covered her half with movie posters. There were hooks in the ceiling, a half dozen of them, that some former tenant had used for hanging mobiles or something, but we used them to hang up sweaters and shirts to dry.

When I opened the door, the first thing Rick did was walk in and get slapped in the face by the tails of a wet shirt.

"Jeez, don't you ever pick up this room!" he exclaimed.

As I had to stand on a chair to loop the clothes hanger over the ceiling hook, the shirt was high enough for Marci and me to walk under without brushing it. I said, "So it's my fault you're too tall?"

I meant it as a joke.

Rick didn't laugh. He sat down on my bed, scowling, and picked up one of my magazines. When he was annoyed, he went dead silent. I let him pout it out. If there's one thing I know about boys, it's that there's no use arguing with them when they're being moody.

I flipped on my ghetto blaster, stuck in one of my favorite tapes, and hummed along with it while I straightened out my nail polish bottles on my dresser top. I loved lining up my bottles of cologne and cosmetics in front of the dresser mirror, so that they reflected themselves into a double row of colored glass. It made me feel as though I owned a department store's whole makeup counter. Everybody's allowed a favorite wishful fantasy, and that's mine.

Allison poked her head in the open doorway. "Anybody here? Oh, there you are!" she said, and then she spotted Rick sitting on my bed. "Oh sorry, didn't know you were busy."

"Come on in," I said, because I could see at a quick glance that she was upset about something. She was pushing her long, straight, pale hair back from her forehead with her fingers in a combing gesture and her hand was shaking. There were red blotches around her eyes.

The last time I'd talked with her, beyond saying hi as we passed in the hallway, was that day in the laundry room when she'd been so upset about her boyfriend, Mark.

"I don't want to bother you," she said.

"That's okay," I said. As I didn't think she'd want to tell me her problem in front of Rick, if the problem was Mark, I added, "Rick was about to go down the hall and get me a soda. You want one?"

For sure I was taking a chance on irritating Rick, but usually he behaved himself when anyone else was around. At worst, he'd walk out without saying a word.

Instead he did his best, sweetest Rick, and said, "Okay, three sodas, huh?" and headed down the hall. He obviously also saw that Allison had been crying.

She flung herself onto my bed, right where Rick had been, and wailed, "I came by a few nights ago to talk to you but your roommate said you couldn't be disturbed, and every time since you've been out and I've got to talk to someone!"

"Sure, honey," I said, "is it Mark?"

"He's dating some girl who lives in Dorrance Hall. I've seen them together, and he hasn't called me in a week, and I'm flunking biology and I think my parents are going to get a divorce and my hair's turning green." Her voice faded away into a soft sobbing.

"I know what you mean," I said. I sat down on my bed beside her and put my arm around her shoulders. "Look, let's go through it one at a time. Mark's done this before, right?"

Allison nodded.

"Okay, for sure it's lousy on you, but you can't change him. Did you try talking to other guys?"

She whispered, "There's a guy in my economics class who keeps following me around, but, Greta, I don't want more problems."

"He doesn't have to be a problem. Go to coffee with him. Talk to him. But don't date him. It'll give you something to think about besides Mark."

"Oh, I don't know."

"Yeah, it's rough. About your parents. You can't do anything about them except keep your fingers crossed. Maybe they'll change their minds. And about biology, I can't help you at all. I've got the same problem in lit. I guess all we can do is keep studying."

"Maybe I should give up and drop out of school and go home," she said.

I gave her a hard look to see how much she meant that. I didn't think that was what she wanted to do at all. But what else I noticed was that she was right, her hair was turning green.

Jumping up, I said, "Know what makes your hair turn green? It's copper, it comes off the water pipes in swimming pools or something like that. My aunt's a hair stylist. If you use a shampoo and conditioner every time after you swim, that helps."

"Or I could dye it blue and be done with it," she said, but although that didn't sound too positive, her voice was steadier.

"Tell you what, that's one problem I can solve. Most of the green is in the tips. Why don't I trim your hair for you?"

"You know how to trim hair?" she said. She was almost smiling.

"Do I ever," I said, because although I am very

short on talent, if there's one thing I know, it's hair. Between my aunt and my beauty magazines, I'd learned hundreds of tricks.

Grabbing up an old school newspaper, I spread it around on the floor, then plunked my desk chair in the middle. With a sweeping bow and wide arm gesture, I said, *"Voilà!* Madame Greta's Hairstyling Salon! Have a seat, miss!"

Allison said, "You sure you know what you're doing?"

"I do my own hair and my mom's hair and I used to do haircuts for friends in high school," I said.

"Honest?" If Allison still looked worried, at least now she was worrying about what I'd do to her hair and not about Mark. That was a big improvement for her mental health, I figured.

I had my combs and brushes and scissors lined up on my dresser top, and a towel tucked around Allison's shoulders, when Rick returned with our three drinks.

"Now what are you up to?" he asked.

"Trimming Allison's hair," I said. I took my soda can from him and set it on the dresser.

"Oh yeah?" he said. He didn't sound especially confident, but he also didn't sound as doubtful as Allison had. I think what he was was curious, because he sat back down on my bed to watch.

"I don't want it short," Allison said.

Handing her my makeup mirror, I said, "Here, you can watch and see what I'm doing, though personally I believe you will be surprised and delighted."

She giggled nervously. Putting the mirror in her lap, she folded her hands on top of it and said, "I don't really want to watch. I'd rather trust you."

Rick snorted.

I grabbed my glass water jar from the dresser and held it out to him. "Go fill this."

"Huh? Where?"

"There's a drinking fountain in the hall," I said.

"Fill a jar in a drinking fountain?"

"Or there's the kitchen on first." There was a small kitchenette off the main hall, so that people could fix snacks, complete with a sink and a new refrigerator and a stove that looked as old and worn out as the linoleum floor.

After he'd gone, Allison said, "I didn't mean to cause your boyfriend a lot of bother."

I said, "You're not. I'm sending him on errands on purpose. It's important to keep guys busy. Let them sit around too long with nothing to do and they get the fidgets."

After fluffing out her hair with my hands, I pushed it around to get the feel of it, then combed it into sections, pinning it out of the way, so that I could unpin one section at a time to trim. Rick returned with the water, handed it to me, and returned to his spectator's spot on the bed, all without a word.

I said, "Thanks so much. Did you go downstairs?"

He didn't bother to nod. We both knew that he couldn't fill that jar in the drinking fountain.

I combed water through the first section of Allison's hair and then positioned the hair on the comb and snipped off the green tips, letting them fall onto the spread newspapers.

She glanced down, saw that I'd cut off less than an inch, and let her shoulders drop, relaxed.

"There now, that didn't hurt, did it?" I said.

She giggled.

"That's all I'm going to take off the back," I said,

"but the sides really should be shorter. Wouldn't you like me to shape it around your face?"

"I don't want to have to set it," she said.

"No, all you have to do is blow-dry it, but if I shape it, it'll fluff out more." ·

"I guess so," she said.

I stood in front of her, put my fingers under her chin, and tilted up her face. "You have great eyes," I said. "If I trim your hair back this way, it'll make them show up more."

"All right, go ahead."

I combed away, snipping only fractions of an inch at a time and stepping back to be sure I liked the effect, humming with the music from my favorite tape as I worked. I love cutting hair. When I'm doing it, I can't worry about anything else.

From the doorway, someone said, "What's going on?"

I swung around.

Inger stood in the hall, watching us.

"Giving her a trim," I said.

"Mind if I watch?" I said I didn't mind and Inger leaned against the doorframe while I continued to comb and snip.

"Some collection you have," she said.

"What?"

"On your door," she said.

"Oh," I said and laughed. The outside of the door was covered with scraps of paper taped to the wood, half mine and half Marci's, a collection of cartoons and newspaper articles and postcards, anything either of us liked and wanted to share with the other girls on the hall.

While Inger read all our cartoons and Rick leafed through a magazine, I finished up Allison's hair.

After the last snip, I combed through all of it again with water, then used my dryer to shape it in place.

At that point I wished that I had one of those swivel chairs, like my aunt has in her shop, so that I could swing Allison around to face a large mirror, but the best I could do was pick up the hand mirror from her lap and hold it in front of her.

"Oh my!" she said, and jumped up and ran over to my dresser, where she looked at her reflection in the larger glass. "Oh, that's wonderful! I love it!"

"Come back after the next time you wash your hair, because there'll be bits that will need to be trimmed," I said.

"You're a marvel," she said.

"I wish my professors thought so," I said. "A talent for cutting hair isn't going to get me through exams."

"You really do have talent," Inger said, her head tilted, her eyes narrowed, as she appraised Allison's haircut.

"Yeah, but it's my one and only," I said.

"Not if that's a self-portrait on the door," she said. "You should be an art major."

As all of the papers on my door were clippings, I didn't know what she was talking about. I'd have asked, except that Allison started saying she should pay me for the trim, and since I'd done it to cheer her, I had to think of some nice way to say no, and then Rick asked when we were going to supper and Allison asked Inger if she was ready to go to supper and they both remembered things that they had to do first.

Shouting "See you later," and "Thanks again," they dashed off.

Rick stood up, dropped the magazine on the bed and said, "You ready to go, now?"

"As soon as I pick up these papers," I said.

"You can do that later," he said.

"No, I can't leave hair all over the floor," I said. "Marci isn't fussy, but that's too much." I stooped down to fold the hair trimmings into the newspapers I'd spread out. While I worked, Rick wandered to the door and stood in the opening reading the cartoons.

I brushed past him and carried the rolled papers down the hallway to the incinerator chute. When I returned, he said, "Who did this?"

He pointed to a drawing taped to my door. I hadn't noticed it earlier, probably because I was so used to our clipping collection, I never looked at it except when I had something new to add.

"Who did what?" I asked.

But as soon as I saw where he was pointing, I knew.

A half sheet of sketch-pad paper was taped among our clippings. On it was a pencil drawing of me, definitely me, done in a cartoon style but leaving no doubt about who it was. It was my long, thin shape, my face, my mass of hair, all collapsed against a mountain of school books.

And the sketching style was the neat, crisp lines that I'd watched David produce in the shapes of insects and birds and fiddlehead ferns.

"I guess it's me," I said.

"I can see that. But who drew it?"

"I don't know. One of the girls, I suppose," I mumbled.

Rick swung around and glared at me. "You have a

girl named David in your dorm?" he snapped. And then he stalked off, leaving me standing in the hallway with my mouth open, while he disappeared around the archway and down the stairs.

I started to run after him. Then I wondered where he'd come up with David's name. Returning to my door, I looked more closely at the sketch.

In very tiny lettering up the spine of one of the books was printed, "David."

David must have dropped by to see me when I was out.

So he knew my room number as well as my phone number.

Thinking of Rick, I almost grabbed the sketch from the door to wad it up and throw it away. But then I looked at it again. It really was clever. In the sketch the little cartoon Greta looked exactly the way I'd felt the last time I'd seen David, overwhelmed by my studies.

It was such a funny little sketch, I couldn't help laughing. David really was a clever artist.

Then I noticed more printing on the other books' spines. One said Cole Hall, another said Langford, and another book spine contained a line of numbers. A phone number.

So his name was David Langford and he lived in Cole Hall and he expected me to phone him. Maybe I'm no detective, but I know enough about boys to figure out that simple a message.

I untaped the sketch from the door, working it loose carefully to avoid tearing it. If I left it on the door, Rick would think David was somebody I cared about. The sketch was too good to throw away. I put in the drawer of my desk to save it, so that I could show it to Marci, and then I ran after Rick.

By the time I caught up with him, he'd picked up his tray in the cafeteria and found a seat at one of the long tables. I sat down beside him.

He didn't bother looking at me. I didn't bother speaking to him. We ate in a total silence that was so thick it practically blocked out all the cafeteria noise, the voices and the scraping sounds of chairs and trays and dishes. Sometimes I could actually imagine a gray cloud surrounding Rick, he could be that horrid.

I gave him until he finished eating to work through his grumpy mood. Then I said, "Can I help it who sticks cartoons on my door?"

"You didn't have to lie about it," he said.

"I didn't! Rick! I didn't even see it until you asked about it, and I didn't see David's name on it until after you left, so how was I supposed to know who drew it?"

"Who's David?" he said.

In a very casual voice, as though it were the most unimportant comment in the world, I said, "Um, I expect it's that guy I bumped into one day, remember, I told you, he was sketching some ferns down by the bridge. At least, he's the only person I know who sketches and is named David."

"So why should he make that sketch of you?"

"I don't know. Maybe he goes around sketching everyone he meets."

"How did he know your room number?"

I could be absolutely honest and look Rick straight in the eye when I said, "I don't know. I didn't even tell him my last name, so that is odd, isn't it? Still, I suppose he could have seen me going into Smith Hall and asked somebody which room was mine."

"How come he's hanging around Smith?" Rick gave me this really cold stare, like he was looking through me and didn't believe me.

"How should I know?" I said, then added quickly, so he wouldn't have time to continue arguing about David, "Listen, they're showing movies upstairs tonight, so if we get up there fast, we can get good seats."

Rick shrugged and I didn't know if that meant yes, he wanted to go to the movie or no, he didn't, but I pretended I thought it meant yes. As we'd first met in the auditorium-theater, I considered it a lucky place.

Jumping up, I said, "Come on, it's one of those spy films, but I can't remember the name," and rushed out.

If there is one thing I know about boys, it's that there is no point waiting around giving them time to continue arguments, because if you do, they will.

So there I was, managing this touchy situation with Rick, rushing along the crowded corridors of the Union building toward the back staircase, when this voice shouted, "Hi, Greta!"

And there by the wall, about ten people away from me, was David the Artist, waving like mad, a big grin on his face.

Rick muttered, "Who's that?" in my ear.

I rushed on by without turning my head, but I did raise my arm to wave over my shoulder, which Rick couldn't see as he was slightly ahead of me. I said, "How should I know?"

"He knows you."

As we headed up the stairs I said, "Listen, Rick, he's probably in one of my classes, but I do not know the name of every guy on campus."

"Yeah, well, they sure all know your name," he said.

As I couldn't think of any answer to that that wouldn't lead to a worse argument, I kept my mouth shut and hoped Rick would love the movie.

Luckily for me, he did.

By the time the film ended, he'd forgotten all about David and the sketch. We walked back to Smith with our arms around each other's waists, on the best of terms.

6

The last week of March started out with that "This is the first day of the rest of my life" feeling. I was in tune with my world. My lit assignments were up to date, my laundry was caught up, my skin was clear and Rick hadn't said a cross word to me in three days. If I mention Rick last, it's because he was so much more important to me than anything else that it scared me. Sometimes our relationship seemed so fragile that I felt as though I had to tiptoe through it to keep it from shattering.

Maybe that's why I was just this little bit nervous when I came swinging up the path at noon from my tennis class and bumped into David. I didn't physically bump into him, not again, but there he was, standing on the bridge, leaning with his back against the railing, very obviously waiting for me.

Sure, he said casually, "Oh, hi, Greta," as though I were the last person he expected to see.

And sure, I said, "Oh, hi, David," as though I believed that our meeting was a coincidence.

But I knew he'd been waiting for me and he knew I knew it.

Most times, I'd have been flattered because having a darling boy stand around waiting to accidentally meet me is a huge compliment, but that particular day my life was humming along so well that I didn't want to chance anything that might upset Rick.

"Going to lunch?" he asked.

It crossed my mind to say that I had laundry to do, but he had this funny look on his face that made me think he was in a mood to willingly agree to tag along and help me with anything I mentioned. And as I didn't have so much as a dirty sweater left in my laundry bag, I didn't think I'd better take a chance on that excuse.

Definitely if I'd said I was going to the library to study, he'd have followed me.

So I silently prayed that Rick had gone to lunch early, which he often did, and was by now well on his way out of the cafeteria.

To David, I said, "Sure."

Honestly, it was not a wildly encouraging sort of reply, and I didn't give him a big smile or bat my eyelashes, or anything, but his already happy-shiny face lit up like a light bulb.

It was impossible not to smile back at a grin like that.

As we walked up the path to the Union building, I said, "I liked the cartoon you left on my door. How'd you know my room number?"

"Looked it up in the student directory. I was going to give the cartoon to you, but when I knocked on your door, nobody answered, and I saw all those other cartoons on your door, so I decided to just leave it."

"But how could you look me up in the directory? You don't know my last name."

"I do, too. Your last name is Greenley."

"How did you know that?"

David stopped walking, faced me and gave me this very teasing grin. "What, you're a secret undercover agent and by learning your name I've broken your code?"

"Right," I said quickly, "so now I'll have to inform the bureau that our passwords have been rendered inoperative."

"I think my stomach is going to be rendered inoperative if I don't get some food in it soon," David said.

We hurried to the cafeteria, joked over the food choices as we went through the line, found a table with a couple of side-by-side empty places, and said our hellos to familiar faces before settling down to our lunches.

David was so easy to talk to, I chattered away at top speed, which for me can be very rapid-fire. Yes, I had one nervous moment, when we first entered the cafeteria. I saw a dark head across the room that I thought was Rick. My breath kind of choked up in my throat, which was dumb, because, honestly, if it had been Rick, why should he give any thought to whom I was standing next to in line? But then it wasn't Rick, and I let my breath out slowly and scanned the huge room and satisfied myself that he wasn't there and relaxed.

I enjoyed myself so much, sharing silly jokes and stories with David, that it wasn't until after he'd waved good-bye and I headed over to my lit class that I realized that he never had told me how he learned my last name.

Was that an accident or on purpose? Boys sometimes like to be mysterious, which I think has something to do with the macho James Bond image thing, so maybe that was it, I decided. Though, truthfully, in no other way did David strike me as the sort of guy who would try to imitate James Bond. Or anybody. Sometimes you meet a person who is so much himself that he doesn't remind you of anyone else. David was like that.

I had supper with Rick. Afterwards, he had to work in the computer room, so I went back to my room to study. But I never quite made it to my books.

Allison was waiting for me, sitting on my bed leafing through one of my magazines, her wet blond hair hanging dead straight.

Marci was at her desk, typing.

Allison said, "You said to come back next time I washed my hair."

"Right," I said, putting my fingertips under her chin to tilt up her face. I squinted and peered at the shape of her cut. "Uh-huh, it needs a little more trimming. I missed a place."

I also noticed that Allison's eyes were red and figured she'd been crying and wanted to talk to me, as much as anything. "Going to bother you if we talk?" I asked Marci.

My nice roommate must also have noticed Allison's eyes, because she said, "Not at all, you go right ahead, I'm just copy typing."

I spread out the papers and settled Allison in the chair, and figured that I'd spend twenty minutes doing a two-minute touch-up trim, to give her time to talk out whatever she wanted to say.

She said, "The haircut is terrific. It's the only terrific thing about me. Everything else is blah."

"That's not true," I said.

"Yes, it is. I look like every other eighteen-year-old in the world. My mother couldn't find me in a crowd. Probably I should make a career of bank robbery, because I could go in without a mask and nobody'd ever remember what I looked like."

"You're underrating yourself," I said, "but still, I know what you mean. I guess we all feel that way about ourselves, sometimes."

"I'll bet you never do," she said so firmly that Marci laughed. Marci has listened to me through my worst downs.

On an up day, like that day, when everything had gone well and Rick had told me how much he hated having to go to the computer room and how much he'd rather be with me, it was hard to remember my down days that well, but I thought about it and said, "The thing is, we're each different but we have to figure out how and then make that special."

"You sound like my mother. There is nothing special about me."

"Sure, there is," I said.

"Give me an example," she said.

"Umm, okay. Listen, have you ever read one of those articles about color? We each have our own color types, see, and when we wear the right colors, we look better and feel better, and when we wear the wrong colors, we get the opposite effect."

"I've heard that, but I am nothing color, that's what I am."

From the doorway, Inger said, "Define nothing color." We looked at her, surprised. She was leaning against the doorframe, one hand on a hip, relaxed, as though she'd been there for a minute or two. She was dressed in jeans that clung to her long legs, and a red sweater that set off her cropped black hair.

Allison said, "Greige."

"You are not greige," I said.

"Then what am I?"

"Umm, let's see, I think you're kind of sunny colors, rose or peach shades, but like me, you can't wear anything bright, nothing like that red sweater. It looks terrific on Inger because she has such strong coloring, but on you or me, all anybody'd see would be the sweater."

"Terrific, I am a sweet little pink nothing," Allison said.

"Yeah," I admitted, "I used to think that, too. We blondes always get dressed in pastels and hair ribbons by our parents, so we grow up feeling like half-melted sherbet cones. What I did, when I first started reading color articles, was switch from baby pastels to adult pastels, you know, like gold and beige and denim blue—well, here, take a look."

I leaned past her and pushed open my closet door. There hung my row of pastel colors on hangers, all beige and ivory and shades of light yellow through gold.

Inger exclaimed, "Your clothes are all the same color!"

"In different shades," Allison said.

I said, "I call them the jungle pastels."

"Jungle! Oh, sure, like your leopard bedspread, beige and gold, and oh my gosh, so are your posters!" Inger said, coming into the room to peer more closely at my posters, which were all in tawny, jungle shades and mounted on dark gold mats.

"How did you decide which color was yours?" Allison said.

"Went to the stores and tried on every color on the racks and took some long, honest looks at myself in the mirrors."

"You should have seen her when she arrived last September," Marci said, talking without looking at us but continuing to type. "Would you believe a Holly Hobbie bedspread and Dumbo bookends?"

Laughing, I said, "That's my mom. In her eyes I shall forever be a pink-ruffles princess. She dressed me in so much pink when I was small that now I can't even look at a strawberry milkshake without gagging."

After I finished with Allison's trim, Inger and I spent another half hour draping my pastels and Marci's brighter scarves and sweaters around Allison, helping her find the real Allison, and then Inger hinted around that she thought her hair had grown out of its cut, so I shaped it up for her, and then Allison and I went back to Inger's room to watch a movie on TV to give Marci some silence in which to type.

About halfway through a movie that wasn't much good, anyway, Marci came running down the hall to tell me I had a phone call.

"Who is it?" I asked as I followed her back to our room.

"It isn't Rick," she said. "Some other guy."

Jon, I figured, and picked up the receiver and said, "Hi."

"Hi, Greta Greenley," David's voice said. Not

that I'd been with him all that much, but David's voice sounded the way David looked, warm and cheerful and not quite like anyone else.

"Hi, David."

"I just remembered that I owed you an answer, and as I didn't want you to sit up all night worrying about it, I thought I should call and tell you."

"Owed me an answer?"

"Thing is," he went on, "in case you do wake in the night and remember that you asked me a question that I never got around to answering, I don't want you to have some nightmare idea that I'm a double agent and really did break your cover—"

"Oh!" I shrieked, and Marci, who had returned to her desk and was working quietly, swung around, startled, to stare at me. "You didn't tell me how you knew my name!"

"Jackpot!" David laughed. "Truth is more boring than fiction, but I'll tell you anyway. I was sitting in my dorm lounge doing that cartoon of you and one of the guys walked by and said, 'What's that?' and I said, 'My friend Greta,' and he said, 'Oh, I know her! That's Greta Greenley!' So that's the answer I owed you."

"Ah hah," I said. "And who was the stool pigeon?"

"I think his name is Pete."

As I knew a couple of guys named Pete, I said, "Well, it goes to prove what good likenesses you do."

"Anything from skunk cabbages to a beautiful woman," he said. "See ya."

And before I could reply to that comment, he hung up.

"Beautiful woman, huh?" I said, more to myself

than to Marci, which was just as well because she didn't hear me over the clatter of her typewriter, anyway.

Now it is always nice to be referred to as a beautiful woman, and who am I to throw away compliments, but it's also one of those things college boys love to go around saying without meaning a word of it. What I liked better was the easy way David had referred to me as "my friend Greta." He hadn't said it to impress me. He'd only been repeating what he'd told Pete, and I don't think he'd even thought about what he was saying to me. So I liked that, that David thought of me as his friend.

"Now what are you daydreaming about?" Marci asked.

She was right. There I stood in the middle of the room staring at nothing. I said, "That was David on the phone. He's crazy but he's nice."

"Oh? What's he like?" she asked.

I started to describe him from a mental picture I had of him, standing by the bridge in his khakis, his light brown hair and skin and sunny eyes all blending with his clothes, and I had to laugh. "He looks like my wardrobe," I said, pointing at my closet with its open door. "He's a blend of jungle pastels."

"*Jungle* and *pastel* sounds like a contradiction of terms to me," she said.

And that is how my up day ended, with a phone call from David. The next day my bubble burst.

After my first morning class, I stopped back at Smith Hall to check my mail, just in case my dad had sent me a check which I'd sort of hinted I could use in my last letter to him, because my allowance had somehow run out.

Anyway, I opened my mailbox, hoping for money

or even a nice letter from home, and instead what I got was an official university envelope. Inside was a notice, one of those horrid computer printout things, that I was flunking lit.

They might as well have sprung open a trapdoor under my feet because that's what I felt like. My mind did a total blank and my heart pounded. I stumbled out of the building, automatically heading over to tennis, but not really thinking about where I was going.

Jon must have said hello to me three times before I realized he was walking beside me.

"Is something wrong?" he asked.

Fighting back tears, I blurted, "I'm flunking lit! It says so right here!"

He took the slip of paper from my hand, studied it and said, "It's a warning notice but it doesn't mean you'll positively fail."

"It doesn't?"

"No, it means you're on the edge at midterm."

"But what can I do?" I wailed.

Jon put his arm around my shoulders and gave me one of his warm hugs. "Come on, Greta, the world hasn't ended. Now calm down. What you do is you go talk to your lit prof after class, and have her go over your grades with you, and see just how far behind you are."

"Far enough to be flunking!"

"Sure, but if that's only for the first half of the semester, and you're simply borderline, find out what sort of grades you need to get yourself back to passing."

What Jon said made perfectly good sense—Jon always did—and by the time we'd finished talking, I was calm enough to go to tennis and anyway, if I was flunking lit, I didn't want to take any chances with any other classes.

As it turned out, I had my best day ever in tennis, because I was so upset I hit that stupid ball as though I was trying to annihilate it, and wound up with some terrific shots.

Afterwards I showered at the gym, I was that hot and steamy, and then headed back to the upper campus to grab lunch before facing my lit class. As I approached the bridge I wondered if David would be waiting for me again. If so, he'd certainly see me in one of my worst moods.

But he wasn't there.

I went on up to the Union building and through the main hallway and had almost reached the cafeteria when Rick hurried over to me, saying, "You're late."

As he hadn't said anything about meeting me for lunch, I couldn't figure what he was talking about.

"I've been waiting for you," he said, and then he gave me a close look and added, "What did you do to your hair?"

What I'd done was that I'd stood under the gym shower and let it run over my head, and then I'd been so upset, still, about that lit notice that I'd forgotten to dry my hair. Until he mentioned it, I hadn't even realized that the ends were dripping all over the shoulders of my sweat shirt.

"What am I late for?" I said. If I sounded apologetic, it was because my self-confidence, like Samson's strength, is in my hair. When it's a mess, so is my personality, my intelligence, everything. All I could think about was how horrible I must look.

"You're usually here earlier, that's all. Listen,

we've got to hurry now so come on," Rick said, grabbing my arm.

"Where are we going?" I said.

"We've got to go to the city library, I need some stuff."

"What's the *we* about? I can't go."

"Will you quit arguing and come on?" he said, pulling on me. His voice was low, so that only I could hear him, but I caught the impatience. There we stood in the middle of the corridor with waves of students pushing past us in both directions, and I suspected we made some sight, this wild-eyed guy glaring at this dripping girl.

"Rick, I've got a class at two and I've barely got time to grab some lunch and I don't want to go without eating because I've got to think straight, I've got to talk to the prof after class—"

"Greta, cut your two o'clock. We'll get something to eat later."

"I can't cut my two o'clock!"

Rick glanced around, suddenly aware that we were in the middle of a crowd. "Come on outside and I'll explain," he said.

I followed him out onto the long steps above the fountain, to a spot where we could look down the length of the campus and see hundreds of people hurrying along the walkways, but we were out of earshot of any of them.

Rick gave me one of his gorgeous smiles, which only made me more aware of how awful I looked, and said, "Honey, the thing is, I lost one of their stupid books, so now they won't let me check out anything until the book is returned and I can't find it, but you can check books out, so I need you to come along and get some books for me that I have got to have today."

"All right," I said, "I can go at four, I should be done talking to the prof then—"

"Greta, I have got to get this stuff now, I've got computer time at four so I have to be back by then—"

"Yes, but Rick I got this notice—"

"And you're wasting time standing here arguing—"

"Let me explain—"

"Greta, unless we get going I am not going to get done in time," he shouted, drowning me out, and I stood there staring at him, my mouth open, realizing that there was no way he was going to listen to my problems or care about them, even though he expected me to turn my world upside down for his, and maybe there were times when I'd have shrugged and said that's how guys are but this time I was already falling apart. I could not pull myself together enough to shrug off a snowflake, much less six feet of shouting male.

All I could manage was to shout back, "No!" and turn and run away from him and down the path to Smith and up the stairs to my room, all in a red-faced, sobbing blur.

When I reached my door I was crying so hard I couldn't find my key. I sank down to the floor and sat with my back against the door and put my face down on my knees and let it all pour out. Fortunately, I was alone in the corridor. Anybody hearing me would have thought I was dying. Matter of fact, that's what I felt like.

Over and over in my mind I replayed that scene on the front steps, with Rick's face reddening, his eyes narrowed, his hand gripping my arm so tightly that I felt bruised. We'd had our fights, sure, but not like that. Before when we'd disagreed, he'd clammed up after a few angry words, then gone off to sulk. But he'd never shouted like that, screaming me down, drowning out my replies, not giving me a chance to explain.

And he'd never grabbed me. Did he know how his fingers had dug into my flesh? Did he know he was hurting me?

I couldn't believe that he did.

He couldn't hurt me, not on purpose.

And when he'd calmed down and I had a chance to show him my failing notice, he'd understand, wouldn't he?

Through the closed door, I heard my phone ringing. Fumbling through my pockets, I finally found my key, unlocked the door and grabbed the receiver off the wall hook, sure that it would be Rick, telling me how sorry he was.

Instead, it was Jon, and what he said was, "I've been thinking about that lit class. You feeling any better?"

"Oh sure," I said, but my voice wouldn't stay steady.

"Are you crying?" he asked.

"It's not just that, it's everything, I've had a big fight with Rick and oh—" My voice broke again. I stopped talking and rubbed at my eyes, trying to push away the tears.

Jon said, "Don't cry, it'll work out. Listen, I've been thinking, maybe you ought to drop that class and take it over next year."

I tried to think through the pounding in my head. "I'd lose all that time, five credits, and then, too,

I've already paid for that class and it's too late to switch to something else."

"Yes, but if you're this upset about it, it isn't worth it."

"Oh, I don't know what to do!" I wailed. "But I can't drop that class, not without trying to pass it!"

"All right, there now, tell you what, if you want to go ahead, why don't you meet me and I'll go to the class with you and afterwards we can talk to your prof and there's bound to be a way to work this out."

When Jon said that, I had this weird flash memory of a time in second grade when I'd gotten in a fight on the playground. I'd hit another little girl in the face. She burst into tears and told the teacher. And the teacher said I couldn't go out on the playground at lunch hour anymore and I was so upset I'd cried all the way home. The next day my mother took me back to school and went in to talk to the teacher.

But I'd been six years old then.

I was eighteen now.

And yet Jon sounded exactly like my mother when she'd said, "Now, Greta, I'll go to school with you and we'll talk to your teacher and we'll work this out."

I bit my lip to stop it from quivering. Then I took a deep breath. And then I said into the phone, "Jon, you're a doll, but I'm okay, really. I'll talk to you tomorrow."

And I said good-bye and hung up.

"Okay, Greta," I said to myself, "glue yourself together." I washed my face, reapplied eye makeup, did a quick steam-curl of my hair ends, and though I still looked like Dracula's bride, I figured at least I looked like her on one of her better days.

That lit prof was going to be more interested in

how well I could discuss the problem than how I looked. As I only had thirty more minutes until class time, I knew I'd better use it to run into the coffee shop for a quick sandwich and a carton of milk rather than spend it rearranging my hair.

I dashed back to my room from the bathroom, grabbed my notebook, pulled my door shut, locked it, and then saw the new addition to our door display.

With only a few lines, David had done his own unmistakable likeness sitting at a coffee shop booth under a clock that read four o'clock.

Underneath the cartoon was penciled, "If you're free."

7

A horrible half an afternoon later, with my life still verging on the brink of disaster, I headed for the coffee shop. It was four-fifteen. My lit prof had said that if I could do B-level work for the rest of the semester, I could pull a low C out of the class. Rick wasn't speaking to me. The March sunshine had faded into a cold gray drizzle. And the only smiling face in my life had probably given up and gone home fifteen minutes ago.

But no. Although the daffodils were bent double under the rain, and the fountain's basin was a shallow swamp of dead leaves, and the Union building's wide steps were deserted, and the corridors were slick with tracked-in mud, David Langford's smile remained sunshine bright. As soon as I rounded the corner into the coffee shop, breathless with running, I saw him across the room, at a far table, waving.

I filled a coffee cup from the machine, dropped my change at the cash register and headed for his table. Coffee sloshed over the rim onto my fingers. I let out a yelp. David took the cup from me, set it on the table and said, "Hi."

"I'm sorry I'm late," I gasped. "I had to stop and talk to my lit prof, I am flunking that stupid course, and she says if I make a straight B for the rest of term I'll pass, but if I'm flunking now, how am I supposed to do that? Still, she could have said I didn't have any chance at all."

"That's true," he said. "So what will you do?"

"Well, I could drop the class."

"Uh-huh."

"And then I wouldn't have that failing grade on my record."

"Sure."

"Only I can't get my tuition back, so that's five hours I'd lose in money, and also that I'd be behind next year."

"That's a lot," he said.

"So what should I do?" I asked.

David leaned his chin on his fist and gazed thoughtfully at me. His eyes were the soft brown of coffee with cream in it and they really did have gold flecks. He said, "I don't know, I think it's one of those things you have to figure out for yourself."

"What would you do if you were me?"

"Oh. That's hard to say. I guess I'd figure out how much time I'd need to get the B, and then see if I really had that much time, and if I didn't, I'd drop it, and if I did, I'd go for it."

"Is that what you'd do?"

"That's not what I said." He laughed, and his face lit up in that funny way. "You asked what I'd do if I were you. You are obviously a sensible person, so if I were sensible you, that's what I'd do. Being me, I'd never have thought through all that stuff about the cost or being credits behind or keeping a failing grade off my record, I'd just have kept muddling through and either pass or fail."

Let me tell you, boys have said many things to me. They've told me that I am pretty, funny, dumb, clever, sweet, spoiled, graceful, klutzy and lots more, but that was the first time one had ever said I was sensible.

It really went to my head.

I sat there in a state of numbness, staring back at him. He didn't seem to mind. He just kept gazing into my eyes.

When I found my wits, I blurted, "I never thought of myself as sensible!"

David said, "How do you think of yourself?"

"I—I don't know!"

"I guess that's one of the most important purposes of college," he said, nodding. "I mean, not to lecture, or anything, but I've thought about that, sometimes wondered what I'm doing here, anyway, especially when I botch up a quiz."

"And what have you decided?" I asked.

"You sure you want to hear all this?"

"Sure, I do."

"See, I figure I'm here to learn about the world, and when I've done that, I'll be better able to know who I am and how I fit into the world."

"But you're so talented! You're an artist!"

"Sure, and I've drawn pictures for my family and friends and for school projects. So that makes me an artistic son, brother, friend and student. But none of that tells me what I'm supposed to do with my life as an adult."

"What do you want to do?" I asked.

"That's what I'm here to find out. And it isn't just what I want to do, because I know I want to do something with art, but it's who I want to be. Some days I feel really ambitious, like I want to charge into the commercial world and make a fortune, and other days I feel like I want to hide away on some island and create the sort of stuff nobody buys."

"Wasn't there some painter who did that, went off to an island?"

"Gauguin," he said.

"And he became very famous."

"All that solitude, he could concentrate on his art."

I had this sudden memory of color slides of Gauguin's work that the art teacher had shown us in high school. I exclaimed, "Solitude! His models were beautiful island women!"

David sat back and let out a yelp of laughter. "Oh, Greta, I hadn't even thought about that!"

"Uh-huh, sure, tell me again about how you're going to spend your life on a deserted island painting skunk cabbages," I said.

For the next hour we sat over our empty coffee cups, trying to sort out our identities and the meaning of life and a whole lot of other serious questions, which always turned into jokes, and by the time either of us thought of checking our watches to see what time it was, the cafeteria was opening for dinner. We went through the line together, sat at a table with friends, finished and left together. Without really planning it, we wandered downstairs to the game room area, where there are pinball machines and video games and a couple of pool tables.

We emptied our pockets of change. I had two quarters and David had three. It took us about ten minutes to lose our whole combined fortunes in a video game machine, that's how talented we both were.

We could hear music from the sound system blaring through the open arch to the rec room, a space at the end of the lower corridor that has a dance floor surrounded by booths. It is sort of the on-campus hangout, and anybody who was bored drifted through it at least once an evening to try to spot friends.

Not that we were bored, we weren't, or at least, I wasn't, but we wandered through the archway and melted into the group of dancers. I don't think either of us said a word about dancing to the other. It just happened. David did some quick dance steps; I imitated him, arm-shrugs and all; he saw that I was imitating and laughed; and then we faced each other and started doing our own interpretations of the music.

At first we were moving fast, swinging around each other, really going. Sometimes we were hardly together at all, then we'd spin and face each other, and occasionally we'd grasp hands in a fast turn. But then the music did a skidding stop and switched to a slow, moody beat and I just naturally moved into David's arms. Right away I liked the way he held me. Some guys kind of grab and hang on, as though they're afraid you'll fall down without their support, their arms rigid, their hands tight. And some barely touch you, so that you have to guess what step they're doing, because they don't give any lead.

With David, his arms felt just right. I knew what he was doing, we were perfectly in step and when I looked at him he was looking at me and smiling back.

If anybody had asked me at that moment whether or not I could ace that lit course, I'd have said, "Of course I can." That's how comfortable and happy I felt inside.

And then David said, "You don't know how much I hate to say this, but I've still got to hit the books tonight."

He was right. I was not going to raise my lit grades on the dance floor of the rec room. Reluctantly, I said as much.

We picked up our notebooks from where we'd dropped them on the table by the door and headed outdoors into the shimmering curtains of spring rain. The sky was dark and the rain formed silver halos around every walkway lamp. We ducked our heads and made a dash for Smith Hall.

At the entrance, David said, "Tomorrow?"

And I said, "Same everything?"

And he grinned, waved, then turned and ran toward his own dorm building, across campus. We both knew that we meant that we'd meet at four in the coffee shop.

I hummed my way upstairs, wandered through the open door of my room, said hi to Marci who was busy working at her desk and then got a look at myself in the mirror.

If I'd looked like Dracula's bride when I'd left the room around noon, now I looked even worse. I let out a shriek.

Marci said, "What's wrong?"

"Look at me! My hair's flunked! My makeup's expired!"

"There's a wastebasket in the corner, if you want to throw yourself away," she said.

"I've been like this all afternoon!"

"No wonder no talent scout spotted you," she said.

"Marci, this is no joke," I wailed. "I have been like this the whole entire time I was with David!"

"How long were you with David?" she asked, looking up from her books to study me.

"Since four o'clock! All through supper! And after, at the rec room! And I looked like this!"

"Did you have him on a leash?"

"Huh?"

"Presumably he could leave, if he was too shocked by your appearance," she said. "By the way, who is David?"

I sighed and sank down on my bed, unable to look at my reflection any longer. When I am a mess, my ego collapses and so does my backbone. "A guy. Nobody special."

"Then what's it matter?"

I tried to think of how to explain that to Marci, but I couldn't. Marci looked the same all the time, slim, pretty, with naturally wavy hair and big dark eyes, and though she could have looked like a model if she'd wanted to spend the time on fixing up, she was perfectly happy going around with her basic self showing. There's no way to explain to people like that what it's like to become less than nobody every time your hair goes limp.

Besides, she was right. It didn't seem to matter to David how I looked. And as I wasn't trying to impress David, it shouldn't matter to me. It wasn't as though I'd been with Rick.

I said, "I don't suppose Rick's phoned?"

"Not since I've been here."

I shrugged and collapsed back on my bed, swinging my legs up against the wall, which is supposed to send blood rushing to the head and improve the complexion, or something like that. "He'll probably never call again."

"Oh? Had a fight?"

"I think it was more like a war," I said.

"You'll make up. You always do."

"Do we? I guess so. Only, I've never seen him this mad. Maybe I ought to call him and tell him I'm sorry."

"Was it your fault?" Marci asked.

"I didn't think so at the time, but I suppose maybe it was. I was so busy worrying about my problems, I couldn't help him with his."

"You can't always help everybody," she said.

"But I could have explained why I couldn't help."

Marci stopped writing in her notebook and swung around in her chair to look at me. I stared back upside down, from where my head was hanging over the edge of the bed. "Greta, if you're going to fret over it all night, why don't you simply pick up the phone and call Rick now and get it over with?"

I couldn't think of any argument for that suggestion, short of admitting that I was a coward.

The worst that could happen would be that Rick was still in a shouting mood. And that's not so bad, over the phone. I could always hold the phone at arm's length.

Getting up from the bed, I said okay to Marci,

took the phone off the hook and dialed Rick. When his roommate answered, I asked for Rick; he said just a sec, and I ended up waiting for eons.

As it is embarrassing to have your roommate know how long your boyfriend keeps you waiting, I rounded the corner of our door and sat down on the floor of the hallway, which was as far as the phone cord reached, and which we both did occasionally when we didn't want to disturb each other with talking. We didn't do it much for privacy. After six months of sharing a room, we didn't have secrets.

Rick finally answered.

"It's me," I said. "I've been worrying about you, if you were able to get that book all right that you needed."

"I got it," he said.

"Oh, because otherwise I could get it for you tomorrow, only, see, today I had to talk to my lit prof. It was really important. I got this notice in the mail." I wasn't explaining myself well. Somehow, when I talked to Rick, my words jumbled and I had an awful time saying what I meant. He made me that nervous. Even as I was talking, my fingers tightened around the receiver until my knuckles whitened.

"It doesn't matter now," he said. "Leanne Chase went with me and checked out the stuff I needed."

Leanne Chase is this gorgeous girl with blue-black hair and a fabulous figure, a tiny girl who barely comes up to Rick's chin. She lives on the third floor of my dorm.

"I didn't know you knew Leanne," I said.

"I know her," he said.

"Oh. Well, that was nice of her. Checking out the books for you, I mean."

"Greta, I've got a lot of studying to do. Did you want something?"

After a put-down like that, there wasn't much I could say except, "No, I guess not."

He hung up. Flat. No good-bye, nothing.

I stared at the phone, considered smashing it against the wall, remembered that it was university property and also was used by my roommate.

As I hung the receiver back on its hook, Marci said, "They're showing a sci-fi movie in the lounge in about three minutes. Want to go?"

"No," I said, staring at the wall so that she couldn't see the tears that I could feel burning at my eyes. "I've got some reading to do."

"Everything okay with Rick?"

"Sure, fine," I said, and did this award-winning job of keeping my voice cheerful. "It's all straightened out."

"That's good," she said. "See you later."

I held in the tears until she'd gone. Then I closed our room door, dived for my bed and pulled my blanket over my head. Huddled beneath the covers, with the world shut out, I prepared for my second major crying jag in one day.

My head ached, my throat ached, my heart ached, but the tears wouldn't come. Mixed in with all my misery over Rick was this expanding fury. I mean, it was rising inside me like milk in a pan on the stove when the heat's set too high. It went right through simmer to scald to boiling over, I was that furious, and two minutes earlier I hadn't even known I was angry.

Throwing off the covers, I strode around my room like some crazy person. I wanted everything out of there that reminded me of Rick. He was not going to put me down that way. I was not going to let him ruin my life.

Digging through my sweater drawer, I found the ribbon from my corsage for the Valentine Dance. I crumpled it up, pretending it was Rick himself, and tossed it in the wastebasket. Taped to my mirror was a heart he'd once drawn on a piece of notebook paper. In its center he'd written our initials. Wham, into the basket with the ribbon. In my desk drawer were some candy wrappers from one rainy afternoon when he'd come over to study with me. Crumple! Wham! And a dried-up ballpoint that he'd left behind and I'd kept because it was his, and the empty plastic case from a cassette tape he'd loaned me, and ticket stubs from a movie, and a paper napkin from a restaurant, and even an empty paper tube from a drinking straw.

How could I ever have been dumb enough to treasure such junk?

I'd even stuck into my wall a couple of thumb tacks that he'd emptied out of his pocket once, muttering something about having used them on his bulletin. I'd treasured them because Rick's very own thumb had pressed against them. Was there another girl in the whole world as stupid as me?

Why would anyone make such a fool of herself over a guy for no other reason than because he looked like a TV star?

And he did.

He not only looked like a TV star, with his marvelous profile and his deep dark eyes and his thick hair and his tall, elegant shape, he even sounded like one. All he had to do was say my name and I was head-to-toe goosebumps.

For one awful moment, I very nearly dug all that junk out of the basket.

Now let me tell you what friends are for. Friends are for showing up when you most need them, even though they don't know that's what they're doing. And that's what happened. They banged on my door and shouted for me.

I wiped at my hot, dry eyes, pushed my limp hair around to no purpose as it would take far more than a push to make it presentable and opened the door to Allison and Inger.

Inger said, "Hey, Greta, want to be on the decorating committee for the April Fool Party?"

"Oh, I don't know," I said, my mind on Rick.

"Too bad," Inger said, "because we already volunteered you."

"Lynne Belmont set up the committee assignments, and freshmen are in charge of painting a mural," Allison added.

Lynne was hospitality hostess for Smith Hall. She was a senior, lived on first floor and took her job very seriously.

"What sort of mural?" I asked.

"The party theme is a Hawaiian luau, so there's supposed to be a big paper mural on the back wall of the lounge that looks Hawaiian. Palm trees, sunshine, like that."

"I can't draw," I said.

"Who can? It doesn't have to be a masterpiece, just a big splash of color," Inger said. "Come on, say you'll do it. At least come on down to the lounge now. We're having a committee meeting to plan the mural."

"Yes, okay," I said, following down the hallway after them. They'd rushed on ahead, sure I would.

We went through the second-floor door to the balcony. From there we could see the far side of the room with the movie screen backed up to the window and the circle of couches filled with people watching a noisy space-odyssey show. Clumping down the stairs, we stood beneath the balcony, staring at the empty wall space, waiting for someone else in the crowd of volunteers to come up with a brilliant suggestion for the mural.

"Maybe we should measure the wall space and figure out how much paper it takes to cover it," Allison said.

"Do we paint the paper before we hang it or after?" Inger asked.

"Unless we've got an artist in the crowd, it probably won't make much difference."

Someone else said, "Anyone can paint a palm tree."

"Yeah, but can anyone else tell that it's a palm tree?" Inger asked.

We joked back and forth about the design, not getting much accomplished other than to agree that the wall needed color. The meeting reminded me of committees I'd been on in high school. We'd talk for days without getting anything done, and then the day of the party, everyone would wander around staring at the place where the project was supposed to be, argue over who was supposed to have done what and then start in working at the last possible moment and somehow put it all together, finishing up as the first guest arrived.

"You wearing a costume?" someone asked.

And the conversation broke into parts, with

Allison and Inger talking wall design, several people discussing what to wear and, behind me, a couple of girls talking about whom to ask.

The party was a week off. By then Rick would be speaking to me again, and maybe by then I'd be speaking to him. I was so torn up over the way he behaved, I kept going back and forth in my mind, one minute thinking I never wanted to see him again, the next hoping he'd phone in the morning and say everything was okay.

One of the voices behind me said, "He keeps following me around, so I suppose I could ask him, but if I do, then he'll think I like him and I'll never get rid of him, will I?"

"Do you want to get rid of him?" the other voice asked.

"What if Harry calls? Then I'd be in a mess, if he was hanging around."

"You think Harry will call?"

"I don't know. I keep thinking he will. He said he would. And if he does, I'd want to ask him to the party, but if he doesn't, I don't want to be stuck without a date. What about you? Who are you going to ask?"

"Oh, I don't know. I sort of thought, well, there's this guy I like, only I thought he was going with someone else. But then today he asked me to go someplace with him."

"He asked you out?"

"Not a date, really, he wanted me to do him a favor, which was okay, but I figured that's all it was, only then this evening he phoned. He didn't ask me out exactly, but he asked about my class schedule and said he'd see me at lunch."

"Sounds like he's trying to work up to asking you out."

"You think so?"

Would you believe that at that point, I almost turned around and told that girl that of course the boy wanted to ask her out, that he was probably shy and that's how shy boys acted. I almost did because that's what a big know-it-all I am about guys, Greta the Expert, forever passing out advice, asked-for or not.

And then she said, "Maybe you're right. I guess I will ask Rick. The worst that can happen—" she went on saying, but I didn't hear the rest.

I was too busy turning very slowly to catch a glimpse over my shoulder without letting her know I was looking to see who she was, and the whole time I was doing this James Bond maneuver, I was thinking, there must be a million guys called Rick.

That's what I was thinking. I was also thinking—because, unfortunately, the human brain is capable of multiple thoughts—that I knew without looking who she was.

Which meant that I also knew that although every third boy on campus might be named Rick, she was talking about *my* Rick.

And I was right.

Behind me, talking away to her friend, her face ducked forward so that her blue-black hair half hid it, was Leanne Chase.

And my Rick was planning to meet her for lunch the very next day.

Oh, he was a great one for memorizing schedules and meeting girls for lunch, I wanted to say out loud.

Who'd know better than me? But I didn't dare open my mouth. For sure I'd never be able to keep my voice friendly and controlled. Instead, I melted my way through the crowd and did my silent disappearing act until I was safely in my room with the door closed where I could kick the wall.

8

Smith Hall's April Fool Party was a campus tradition. It had the reputation of being one of the best dorm parties of the year. To attend, you had to be invited as the guest of a Smith Hall resident, and as Smith was a women's dorm, it was a girls-ask-the-guys party.

All of the dorms gave parties at one time or other during the year. And all of the parties were popular, but many of them were little more than open houses, with refreshments set up in students' rooms, as well as games and dancing and movies, so that people wandered through the corridors from room to room. Very informal and unplanned.

None of that stuff for Smith Hall, probably the best-organized dorm on campus, maybe because it was the women's dorm. We had officers and committees and subcommittees and planning councils, and when someone wasn't putting up decorations, they were taking them down. I'm not sure if this had always been Smith Hall's style, but certainly the hall had never missed decorating for a season or holiday since Lynne Belmont, our current hall president, had moved in, and she'd been living in Smith for four years, since her freshman year.

Now I am not going to pretend that Lynne Belmont is one of my favorite people. Sure, I try to like everyone, but some people are harder to like than others.

Marci says that I am unfair about Lynne and I am sure Marci is right, but to explain my side I've got to describe what happened the morning after I overheard that rotten conversation between Leanne and her friend.

After a wretched, sleepless night, I knocked my radio alarm clock on the floor turning it off. As I grabbed to catch it, I was so entangled in my sheets that I fell out of bed.

From under her covers, Marci mumbled, "You okay?"

I mumbled back that I was. Then I lay on the floor until I could rouse myself enough to unwind from the blankets. Staggering to my feet, I tried to right the radio, dropped it a second time and decided to let that go until later. Grabbing my towel and washcloth and soap and toothpaste and toothbrush, which I did by feeling my way around the room and jamming the smaller items into the pocket of my pajama top, I fumbled my way through the door and groped along the hall toward the bathroom.

My eyes were narrow slits, through which I could barely make out shapes of light and shadow, and that's all the way they would open.

My mind remained asleep.

Into all this bleakness soared a cheerful, bright voice, singing out, "Greta, I am *so* pleased to hear that you're going to be on the decorating committee! I know you've been too busy to do committee assignments before, but I do think everyone should work on at least one committee, just for the experience, and I know you'll be wonderful!"

Uh-huh, it was Lynne Belmont.

I tilted my head to improve my vision through the slits. Lynne looked as perfect as she sounded. Now I don't want to be nasty about this, but there is something obscene about a person who has all her makeup done, her hair curled and is neatly dressed in a knockout outfit by six-thirty in the morning, especially when that person is a naturally gorgeous redhead.

I managed to croak, "Sure, right."

She said, "I know you're in a hurry so I won't keep you now, but I did want to tell you how delighted I am to have you on our party committee."

Maybe I would have been more receptive to Lynne's enthusiasm if I'd had any reason to look forward to the party. But as it was, I'd spent a night drifting between confused nightmares of myself crouched on the balcony peering down through the banister at Rick and Leanne, standing below me in a dimly lit lounge, their arms wrapped around each other.

Was she really going to ask Rick to the dance?

My head ached at the thought. Stepping into the shower, I let it go full blast. For sure it woke me up. And as soon as I was awake, I realized that I'd forgotten to bring my robe, which meant I had to put my pajamas back on to return to my room, which put me a couple more minutes behind schedule.

Back in the room, I dressed and set to work on my hair. Sometimes that's my best thinking time, staring at myself in the mirror while I hold the dryer. Today all I could see was tall, skinny me, too pale to notice, with huge pores and invisible eyelashes. Leanne was certainly my opposite, small and dark and curvy, with huge eyes and invisible pores.

I thought maybe I should phone Rick immediately and ask him to the party before Leanne could.

But then, if she asked him later in the day, would he be sorry he'd accepted my invitation?

Or would he say no to me to start with, hoping she'd ask him?

I wanted to die or scream or kick something. Instead, I kept right on putting myself together. And my thoughts went right on stirring through every remembered conversation, trying to sort things out.

Leanne had said that Rick had been waiting around for her, hadn't she? That meant he was interested in her. So even if he went to the party with me, he'd be wishing he was with her.

Or was I being foolish in my jealousy? Maybe he wasn't the least bit attracted to her and had only used her to get those dumb library books checked out.

By the time I headed over to the Union building for breakfast, I hadn't solved a thing. I still was totally confused.

Inger waved me over to her table as I went through the cafeteria line, pointing to an empty chair. I sat down next to her. The cafeteria was always quietest at breakfast. It was more than half-empty, and the people who did make it to breakfast were seldom wide awake.

Inger leaned toward me and said, "Where did you disappear to last night?"

"Sorry, I had to leave."

"You're not going to drop off the committee?" she asked.

"Too late for that," I said, and told her about my morning encounter with Lynne.

Inger said, "It'll be a great party and you'll be glad you helped."

"I don't mind helping," I said. "But I'm not sure if I'll go to the party."

"How come?"

If she hadn't asked, I wouldn't have said a word, but as she had, I blurted out what I'd heard Leanne say.

Inger said, "That's not like you, Greta! Where's the girl who isn't going to let a guy push her around?"

"He's not pushing me. He's ignoring me."

"So you have to let him know you have your own life and that you don't care!"

"I hate it when people give me back my own advice and I can't follow it," I said.

"Why can't you?" Inger was one of those girls who didn't give up. I should have guessed that, from her sleek appearance. She didn't have a misplaced pound on her slender, long-legged frame. Her short black hair always gleamed in place. And her thin, intelligent face had a perpetual expression of self-discipline.

"What am I supposed to do?" I asked. "If I ask him and he turns me down, I'll feel rotten, and if I ask and he says yes, I'll worry that he'd rather go with her."

"Why not ask someone else to the party?" Inger said.

"And then what if he's really waiting for me to ask him and has no intention of going with Leanne? That'd end us for sure."

Inger frowned, a deep crease forming between her eyebrows. "I see your point."

"Don't you let it wreck your day. Mine's already shot, so I might as well keep it my problem," I said.

"Wait a minute, tell you what I could do," she said slowly. "I'll see Leanne sometime today, or if I don't, I'll make it a point to see her this evening, and I'll ask her who she's invited to the party. Then I'll let you know."

"That's nice of you," I said.

Inger said, "No, it's not. Next time I'm having a problem with my boyfriend, you can do as much for me."

"Deal," I said.

We finished breakfast, carried our trays to the clean-up counter, said so long and headed for our morning classes. As I walked toward my nine o'clock, Jon fell into step beside me. I smiled up at him. It wouldn't do to let Jon see that I was worried. He'd feel required to give me a long pep talk and I didn't have time for that.

"Have you made a decision about your lit class?" he asked.

"I talked to the prof like you suggested and I think I can pass if I really work at it."

"Good," he said. "Now what you need to do is set up a regular study schedule, allow a set time every day. I'm pretty good at lit. I can drill you for quizzes.

And I know a couple of guys who are English majors. They can go over your papers."

Why did Jon remind me more and more of my mother? I said, "You're an angel, you really are. But there are some lit majors in my dorm. They'll help me."

"All right, but you know you can call me. Any time."

"I will if I need to," I said, blew him a kiss and turned and fled toward my classroom building before Jon could organize me any further.

At noon I ran into Marci and Allison in the cafeteria lunch line. Allison was all smiles. Either Mark had phoned her or she'd aced a quiz. I decided not to ask which. Thing is, if she was up about a quiz, I didn't want to knock her down reminding her of her problems with Mark.

Instead we talked about the decorations for the party. Allison said, "It's a Hawaiian theme and I don't have anything Hawaiian to wear."

"What! No grass skirt in your wardrobe?" I said.

"Not so much as a Hawaiian print shirt," she said.

"How about beach gear?" Marci said, ever practical. "I figured I'd wear a bright T-shirt, white shorts, sandals."

"That sounds okay," Allison said, adding, "I guess we know what Greta will wear?"

"What?" I asked, having no idea what she had in mind as I hadn't given it a thought. I was too busy wondering if I was even going to be attending the party and with whom.

"Jungle pastels," she said and giggled.

"Maybe you could wear a bikini, clunky jewelry, back-comb your hair into a mop and go as a Frazetta poster," Marci said.

"I could take my tray and go eat my lunch alone in a corner," I said. "Then you two would be free to continue making hilarious jokes at my expense."

"You don't have to leave. We'll make jokes about you in front of you," Allison said.

"What else are friends for?" Marci said.

And then Allison said, "Mark said something about wearing matching outfits for the party. You think that'd be all right?" which explained her cheerful mood.

Even though my own love life was in tatters, I was happy for Allison. Besides, maybe I was wrong. Maybe Inger would find out that Leanne had asked Rick to the party and he'd turned her down, never having had any intention of going with anyone but me.

I hung onto that positive thought right through lunch.

Inger hailed me on the way to my two o'clock, standing above me on the upper path. I turned back and climbed the slope. She ran toward me.

Out of breath, she gasped, "Can't stop, I'm late, but I did ask Leanne when I saw her this morning and I hate to tell you this but I might as well get it over with. She phoned Rick last night, must have done it right after you heard her."

From Inger's expression I knew very well what it was that she didn't want to tell me. I said, "And he's going with her."

Hands on hips, Inger put on her determined expression. "Now, Greta, it's no good throwing your heart after some guy who's not worth it."

"Maybe he's worth it," I blurted.

"Stop that! Shape up! Shoulders back! Go ask someone else!" she shouted.

At least we were outdoors on a side path, shielded from the main walkways by the shrubberies. I could have run into her in the cafeteria and had her straighten out my life at the top of her lungs in front of the whole student body.

I mumbled, "Yeah, well, thanks for finding out."

As I headed away from her toward my lit class, she called after me, "It's what *you'd* tell *me* to do!"

She was right. And that's the whole trouble with advice. It's easy to hand out but hard to follow.

I'd have gone off somewhere by myself to have a good cry if my next class hadn't been lit. Flunking lit would not only not get Rick back for me, it would remove me from college and from any hope of seeing him again.

After lit class I remained at my desk, copying some authors and titles of suggested outside reading that the prof had written on the blackboard. By the time I finished, I was alone in the room. Flipping through my notebook, I began to see what Jon meant about putting things in order. My lecture notes were a jumble, having no chronology. Authors' names were scattered. If I went over each name with my highlighter, I could then go back and organize my notes, I realized. Highlighting away, I was surprised when a janitor came into the room.

"Hi," I said in answer to his nod. Glancing at my watch, I saw that it was four-ten. And then I remembered that I'd promised to meet David at four.

I'd totally forgotten David.

And only a day ago I'd had such a wonderful time with him.

Yes, but that was back when Rick was my boyfriend and I thought our fight was temporary like all the others. That was back when David was simply a darling friend to get me through a difficult afternoon.

And that's what he'd done. For a few hours I'd forgotten about Rick and had a good time. Standing David up now was hardly the way to treat a friend.

Gathering up my books, I raced across the campus to the Union building's coffee shop. If he'd given up and gone off without me, I wouldn't have been surprised.

But he hadn't. He was waiting. Smiling.

I slid into the chair across from him, propped my elbows on the formica table top, waited a second for my breathing to slow and blurted out, "I'm sorry, honestly, I stayed to take some notes and I'm really going to have to spend the rest of today studying, I'm so much behind."

David said, "Hi, Greta."

"Hi, David," I said. I'd meant to apologize further for keeping him waiting. It wasn't necessary. Without his saying anything else, I knew that. He understood why I was late.

He said, "I should be working on my botany charts. It's nice out. You want to go down to the bridge with me? Can you study there?"

"That's maybe the quietest place on campus," I said.

I had meant to beg off and go back to my room alone. On the dash from my classroom to the coffee shop I'd had time to think about David.

What I'd thought was this: I was letting David become more than just another guy to be seen eating lunch with. I was letting him move into my life. In no time he'd be like Jon, waiting for me, following me around, telling me how to run my life. I didn't need another big-brother figure.

So why did I agree to study with him? I wish I knew. Tossing away my good intentions, I picked up my books, went by the service counter with him to pick up a couple of milkshakes in cartons, and then headed down the path to the grassy area on the far side of the bridge.

David was right. It was nice out. I hadn't even noticed what the day was like, I'd been so busy with my other worries, until we settled down on the warm, dry grass. We'd wandered along the stream's edge for a few yards, out of sight from the path, to a soft patch of lawn beyond the ferns and beneath an alder. Its trunk shone dappled silver in the sunlight that filtered through its shimmering new leaves.

I spread out my papers around me, poked the straw through the hole in the milkshake container lid, and settled to the job of organizing my notes. Beside me David stretched out on his stomach, propped himself up on his elbows, and concentrated on his open notebook of botany charts.

The sun warmed the top of my head.

David shifted position beside me.

The authors' names overlapped each other in a confused chronology. I frowned at them and kept working.

David rolled over onto his back and gazed up at me, the sun in his face. He raised his arm to shield his eyes and squinted through the narrow shadow. "Have you ever had any botany?"

"No. Hit a problem?"

"Have I ever!"

"Sorry," I said. "I don't suppose you've taken Lit 103 yet?"

"Nope," he said.

We were equally useless to each other as tutors. Having determined that, David sat up, pulled his notebook onto his knees, and bent over it, his forehead drawn into frown lines of concentration.

I really liked the way David's emotions showed so clearly on his face. It was like watching someone's thoughts written out on a video screen.

"How are your other classes going?" I asked, now that he'd interrupted me.

"Shh," he said, not really at me, but at the whole world, staring at his book. Something had begun to make sense to him and he didn't want to lose the thought.

I returned to my own confusing notes, rearranging pages and recopying information that was out of order. And at about the point that I was sure that it would never make sense, something snapped into place and I saw how the chronology affected the writers' works and why that was important.

And I think David said something and I know I said *shh* and twenty minutes later I looked at him and laughed and shouted, "I've got it!"

"Got what?" David asked.

"The whole point of the prof's lectures! *Now* I see what I was doing wrong on the quizzes and on my last paper!"

"That's great," he said.

"This place must be inspirational!" I cried, waving my arms at the marvelous bright blue sky.

"In that case, I'd better do all my studying here," he said.

"You still having trouble?"

"It's better," he said. "No major breakthrough, but the first small glimmer of comprehension."

"I'm sure you're on the verge of inspiration," I said.

"Yeah," he laughed, "but know what? Glimmers of comprehension work up terrible appetites and the cafeteria opened for dinner a half hour ago."

"Why didn't you say so?"

"I did, half an hour ago, but you were wavering on that verge you mentioned and I didn't want to interrupt."

As we gathered up our books and headed for the cafeteria, I said, "That's sweet, a guy who'll silently suffer through hunger pangs for me."

"That's my How-to-Attract-a-Woman Technique Number Three," he said.

"What is?" I stopped in the path to stare at him.

"Suffering through hunger pangs. Creates a real martyr image."

"Martyrs are a bore," I said.

"Cross that out. Let's see, would it bring out the mother instinct?"

"It might in my mother. Not in me."

"Maybe I'd do best to toss out Technique Three altogether."

"Well," I said slowly, "I did find it attractive so it must have some value."

"Care to analyze that?"

"All right, I guess what I appreciated was your patience rather than your hunger."

"Ah! So that's the secret! Maybe that should be

my Technique Number One, display inordinate amounts of patience!"

Realizing how accurately that rule applied to any guy who wanted to impress me, I giggled. "Definitely Technique One with girls who are always late."

"Are you always late?"

"I don't mean to be. Do you always conduct your relationships according to a list of techniques?"

"You're my trial run," he said.

"What! You mean I'm some sort of experiment?"

"No, of course not!" I'd been teasing but David looked honestly worried, as though he really believed that I thought he was using me to practice his attracting-women techniques.

Continuing on up the path, I left David to run to catch up with me. Then I said, "I understand perfectly, Mr. Langford. I am your late afternoon guinea pig. No doubt you also have a morning subject and a late evening subject and maybe even a noon subject."

"Greta!" he tried to interrupt.

"What did you say your university major is?" I continued. "Psychology? Women's Studies? Or just women?"

"Greta," he said, flatly, no question mark, no explanation point.

"Greta what?" I said, and stopped walking, because he'd put his hand on my arm to stop me.

"That's what I'd like to major in," he said.

A comment like that is very hard to answer, especially when it is said in a low, serious voice. Add to that this nice, solemn face, with warm brown eyes gazing at me in a terribly sincere manner. What could I do? If I made a joke, I was afraid he'd be hurt and it would show all over his face and I'd feel about two inches high.

So instead I gazed right back and said, "Would you like to go to the Smith Hall April Fool Party with me?"

9

It took me the next three days to decide what to wear to the April Fool Party. I don't mean that I actually stood in front of my closet grabbing out handfuls of clothes and spreading them on my bed, trying to decide. That's my thirty-minutes-before-time-to-go approach. And I went to my classes and did my assignments and carried out all the other routines of my life, including the weekly letter to my parents.

But nagging at the back of my mind, and popping into the front of it whenever I wasn't actively thinking of something else, was the question, *What to wear?*

And so naturally it became the main conversation topic with the other girls in the dorm. They brought it up as often as I did.

Inger, who is clever with her hands, put together a

grass skirt of crepe paper streamers and made a lei to match.

When she showed it to us, standing in her room and wearing it over shorts and a red halter top, Allison wailed, "If I made one of those things, about halfway through the party the streamers would fall out."

"That's one way to hold Mark's attention," Inger said. She turned in front of her mirror, checking the effect. The skirt did a super job of showing off her long legs.

Unhooking the grass skirt, she held it out to me. "Let's see how it looks on you, Greta."

I fastened it on over my shorts. The effect was not the same. I said, "Inger, if I had your legs, I'd stay up all night putting one of these things together; but face it, the way it looks on me, it's not worth the bother."

After I'd removed the skirt, I held it out to Allison. She shook her head and pushed nervously at her pale hair with her fingers. "No, I don't think so. What I'd like is a sarong. You think I could wrap a peasant skirt into a sarong?"

"Get your skirt and let's see," Inger said.

When Allison left to run down the hall to her room, Inger said to me, "I'm glad you asked another guy. No way should you let Rick think you'll wait around for him while he dates other girls."

"I didn't ask David to make Rick jealous," I said.

Inger's eyebrows shot up in disbelief. "Didn't you?"

"No. Honestly. David's nice, I enjoy being with him and I figured he'd like the party."

"That the only reason?" she prodded.

I said firmly, "He is not my type because as you

and I both know, I am only attracted to bums and creeps."

Allison returned with her peasant skirt, a flowered print with a ruffle that looked more like a square dance skirt than something Hawaiian. She stood in front of the mirror frowning at it while Inger pinned and pulled it around. The skirt bunched out around Allison at weird angles no matter what Inger did.

"It won't work," Allison groaned.

"It doesn't really look like the right kind of print for a sarong, even if you could get the shape right," I said.

Inger said, "Sarongs are nothing more than flat pieces of material. We can't flatten this properly because of the way it's gathered to the waistband."

"Wait a sec," I said, and dashed down the hall to my room, pulled my leopard-spotted cover sheet off my bed and dashed back.

Inger said, "It's worth a try," and folded it over to half the size, then draped it around Allison.

She did a good drape job, but it still wasn't right. Allison turned in front of the mirror. "I like the style, but do they have leopards in Hawaii?"

Inger said, "No, only in Greta's private jungle."

"Try it on Greta," Allison said.

The two of them draped my sheet around me. It did about as much for me as the grass skirt had done. "Hawaiian is not my style. But I like it on you, Allison. What you need is a different print."

"And less cloth," Inger said. "Okay, let's go out to the mall tomorrow and buy cloth."

"That still doesn't settle what I'll wear," I said.

"Oh, you!" Inger laughed. "We already know."

In unison, Allison and Inger shouted, "Jungle pastels!"

So of course my subconscious kept nagging at me to think of something different to wear.

By the Friday before the party I still hadn't made any decision. And Friday night, I didn't have time. Allison and Inger and Marci and I spent the first half of the night standing around listening to everyone argue about what to paint on the backdrop and the other half of the night hanging the paper and painting, naturally, palm trees and a sunset.

But at least everyone had their say.

We trudged off to bed at three A.M., stiff and paint-covered. We did manage to pull off our stained shirts and jeans before getting into our beds, but that was all.

"If we don't wash our faces, they'll fall off," I muttered to Marci.

From her bed across the room, she muttered back, "Let them fall."

I spent a good half minute seriously thinking about getting up and going down the hall to the showers, and wondering how much permanent damage my complexion would suffer from missing one night's washing. My face lost. Shutting out my terribly guilty conscience, I pulled my covers over my head and went to sleep.

But I made up for it Saturday. I spent most of the morning in the shower. Actually, that's an exaggeration, but it is what Marci said when I finally returned to our room in my bathrobe, my hair dripping.

"You've been in the shower all morning," she said.

"It takes some of us longer to get beautiful," I said.

"Have you decided what you're going to wear?"

Shaking my head, I stood in front of my open closet door. Nothing looked Hawaiian. And if it did, it wouldn't look decent on me. I'd tried on the grass skirt and I'd even given sarongs a second chance, trying on the one Inger put together for Allison from material they found at the mall. It looked terrific on Allison. On me it was awful.

I pulled clothes from their hangers and spread them around the room, trying to match up something. I must have done a lot of mumbling, because Marci finally said, "Maybe you're worrying too much. Really, you can wear anything casual. It's not a costume party."

"Everyone else will be going Hawaiian. I'll be going *plain Greta.*"

She said, "You need a confidence boost? You want me to tell you that you never look plain?"

Staring at my freshly scrubbed, unmade-up face and my straight, wet hair, in the mirror, I said, "Please do. Nobody will hold a white lie against you."

What I finally did, after spending most of the day setting my hair and doing my nails and taking a boring study break to review for Monday's quiz, was dress *Greta.* Maybe not *plain Greta,* but definitely *Greta.* I decided that if I didn't look good in a Hawaiian costume, I might as well wear something in which I did look good, otherwise it would be a terrible waste of all that hair spray and nail polish and makeup.

Not that the decision was easy. First I pulled on jeans and a T-shirt and my leather jacket with the studs.

Marci said, "You'll pass out from the heat in that."

She was right, of course. I dropped my jacket and shirt on the floor and pulled on a sweatshirt that has a big lion's face printed on the front of it.

Marci'd disappeared so I stepped out into the hallway to find her.

Somebody let out a shriek, but then, people were always shrieking so I didn't think too much of that, and then Inger dashed toward me shouting, "Greta, help, come on!" and dragged me back into my room.

"What's the matter?"

"My eyebrows won't work! I want them thick and dark, to look really good, and I have these new eyelashes but I can't make them stick!"

"Let me see them," I said.

"Wait here, I'll get them."

"Listen, what do you think of this shirt?"

"Lions in Hawaii?" she said, and dashed out.

I changed to a flowered shirt while she found her eyelashes. When she returned, I put them on her for her and did her eyebrows.

"That shirt is better," she said.

"Think so? I dunno, my mother sent it to me and I guess it's okay but I've never worn it because I'm not real crazy about it." I started to follow Inger into the corridor.

She practically knocked me over, spinning around and shoving me back into my room, saying, "You're right! You are! I can see that now! That shirt is not *you!* Find something else."

Next I tried on a yellow cotton knit top with my tan shorts. Turning in front of the mirror, I thought I looked okay but somehow not right and, totally confused, I headed out of my room again to look for Marci. When I couldn't see her in the hall, I thought she might be in Allison's room.

I knocked on Allison's door. Allison started to throw it open, then pushed it closed, practically catching me in it, and peered at me through the crack.

"What do you want?" she said, which made me feel like I might be carrying some plague.

"I just wanted to ask what you thought of this outfit."

"Oh!" She looked really startled, almost guilty, as though she were hiding something in her room. She blurted, "Uh, yeah, no, looks like you're going to play tennis."

"Umm, that's what I was afraid of," I said.

"Find something else," she said, and closed her door.

Heading back to my room, I bumped into Inger dragging a laundry bag down the hall.

"You doing laundry now?" I asked. "You don't have time."

She said, "Oh, I'm in no hurry, I don't have a date for the party, anyway, so it doesn't matter if I'm late."

And then Marci popped out of Inger's room, said, "Greta, you'll never be ready if you don't hurry up," and practically dragged me back to our room.

So I went back and changed one more time.

I wore my favorite khakis, the ones with the brass snaps on the pockets plus heavy ankle zippers. And my beige mesh shirt. And my pale gold silk scarf. And my extra-long bead-and-copper earrings.

Marci said, "I hope you're completely satisfied with that outfit now."

I spun to face her, my atomizer of gardenia cologne in my hand. "Is it too terrible?"

"You look wonderful," she said.

"You're just saying that," I said. "You're the one who looks wonderful." She did in her red shirt and white shorts. They showed off her slim figure and dark coloring.

She assured me, "You really do look fine. And if you take one more thing out, I won't be able to find the door."

Half the contents of my closet and drawers were strewn across both beds and chairs. I let out a shriek of shock, because, honestly, I hadn't realized I'd pulled out *that* much, and grabbed up armfuls. Racing around the room, I jammed stuff back into drawers and onto wall hooks, and kicked several odd shoes under my bed.

"Let it go till tomorrow," she said. "The guys are probably already in the lounge."

"What time is it?"

"Five-thirty," she said.

"I told David I'd meet him at five!"

"That's going to be hard to do," she said in her ever-calm Marci tone as I raced past her and down the hallway.

The dorm looked like the ticket line for a rock concert, there were that many people milling around. Everyone was shouting to someone else, usually someone half a room away. They were dressed in an assortment of outfits, from shorts and jeans with tops, to all-out Hawaiian costumes of grass skirts and straw hats, to the most formal of couples who showed up with the guy in a white tux and the girl in a long, flowing, very gorgeous muumuu.

Colored crepe paper streamers tied from the balcony to the far wall of the lounge formed a rainbow ceiling of rose and yellow and blue and lavender. All of the couches were draped with flowered print bedsheets. By the far doors that led to a patio area behind the dorm, there were enormous plastic palm trees. And out on the patio was a real sailboat, ten or twelve feet long, its sail rustling in the warm evening breeze. The boat itself was filled with ice and canned drinks. Next to it were the barbecues, the portable metal kind, giving off fantastic clouds of charcoal and hamburger aromas.

And standing on the far side of one of the barbecues, spatula in hand, turning hamburger patties above the flames, was David. He was wearing shorts and a sweat shirt, with the sleeves pushed up above his elbows. His face was flushed from the heat.

I shouted his name.

He looked up, saw me, grinned.

Beside him, Inger said, "Keep working!" I was surprised to see her. She must have changed her mind about doing laundry.

He gave her his nice smile, but he also handed her the spatula and left to walk around the barbecues and join me.

"Quitter!" she shouted after him.

"I'll be back," he said to her, and then to me he said, "Hi."

"I'm sorry I'm late," I said.

"I was early," he said.

We circled the room, saying hi to friends. Some were a trifle hard to recognize beneath flower-covered black wigs. Remembering that Marci had never actually met David, I led him through the crowd toward her. She was standing in front of our mural, pointing at it and saying something to Steve, her steady.

Now I want to make it clear that I have nothing against Steve. In fact, I would highly recommend him to anyone but Marci. He is exactly the sort of boy a girl should look for, nice-looking in a neat, well-groomed way, except for Steve's hair, which is so straight that it continually slides into his eyes no matter how often he combs it back. He's average tall and average smart, or maybe above average on that one, and has an average charming personality. Because he's not a jock or a glamour boy, he doesn't expect girls to swoon at his feet, and so he's just naturally polite and thoughtful. A perfect guy, in every way except one small flaw.

He and Marci went to high school together. They come from the same home town.

Now, honestly, as I've said to Marci a thousand times, what's the point of going away to college if you're going to date a guy from your own home town?

When I'd introduced everyone, Steve said, "Which part of the mural did you paint, Greta?"

I said, "The rose and lavender stripes in the rainbow."

Steve said, "Best rose and lavender stripes I've ever seen," proving that he was a really nice guy.

David said, "How many rose and lavender stripes have you seen?" proving that my methods of evaluating guys are not infallible.

"I expected you to be at least as polite a liar as Steve," I told him.

Marci said, "No art major could look at that mural and say something nice."

As even I, who am not artistic, could see that although the mural was large and bright, it displayed the quality level of kindergarten work, I forgave David.

"Come on, let's eat before the starving hordes find the food," I said.

Returning to the patio, we picked up our plates and went down the food tables, helping ourselves to pineapple baked beans, spiced applesauce cake, a half dozen different kinds of salads and then, from the barbecue, hamburgers on buns and piled with barbecue sauce, pickles, mustard, onions and lettuce.

Some people piled their hamburgers higher than others of us, as I pointed out to David.

"That's the best part, the pickles and stuff," he said. "I only take the hamburger to give me something to put the rest on."

We sat on the lawn, crushed in among everyone else, with people on the outside getting the drinks from the sailboat and passing the cold, wet cans through the crowd to those of us in the center.

We were packed so tightly together that as we sat cross-legged on the grass, David's knee overlapped mine and our elbows kept tangling. I bumped him and knocked the beans off his fork.

"Here," he said, holding out a forkful of salad toward me, "maybe it would be easier if I fed you first, and then you can feed me."

"Or we could feed each other at the same time," I said.

"Impossible," he said.

"Is that a challenge?" I asked.

Ever try to eat off a fork someone else is holding

while holding out a forkful of food to him? It was a good thing we started with the salad instead of the beans.

"Your aim is terrible!" David sputtered, brushing lettuce from his bare knee.

I reached out and wiped salad dressing off his chin. "This would be easier if you'd stop laughing."

"Reminds me of the games we played at birthday parties when I was little."

"Funny, I never think of boys as going to birthday parties," I said.

"You think only girls have birthdays?"

"I guess I was thinking of the kind of birthday parties my mother gave for me. She'd dress me in ruffles and a huge hair bow, and she'd fix up the table like a ladies' luncheon, with paper lace decorations, and invite four or five other ruffled little girls."

"On your next birthday I'll have to give you a proper party, with tug-of-war and water pistol fights and arm-wrestling and egg-on-a-spoon races—"

"My heavens! You sound like a guy who really knows how to celebrate a birthday!"

As people finished eating, they divided into a variety of activities. On the patio Tim Canfield was organizing a game of charades. I tried to spot his date, but I couldn't figure out who he was with. Not that it mattered, but I was curious because although he was nothing to me, Marci's cousin Joanne had been crazy in love with him.

I shouted, "Hey, Canfield, making up new rules for the game?"

He looked through the crowd, saw me, waved and shouted back, "I'll play by your rules any time, gorgeous!" which was a truly Canfield reply.

David and I picked our way through the crowd to

return to the lounge where a dance band had begun to strum Hawaiian melodies. They wore white pants, flowered shirts and paper leis, and their instruments included three guitars, a ukelele and drums. One of the guitarists also played piano. And they all sang, even the drummer, being typical multitalented music majors.

Marci and Steve and Inger were in a noisy discussion group that had collected on the balcony. In a corner of the lounge Allison and Mark were deep in a very private conversation. I couldn't tell how that was going, but for her sake, I hoped it was romantic.

We moved into the growing throng of dancers, David leading to open a path, doing dance steps and swinging his shoulders in time with the beat. I followed, imitating him. When he found an open place, he turned to me and we circled each other, picking up the rhythm. He was a terrific dancer.

Some guys dance because they think it is one of those things they have to do as part of dating girls, and some guys dance because they love to dance. Anybody watching David could see that he was that second kind of guy.

His smile lit his face. His eyes sparkled. And although we weren't touching each other, so he wasn't actually leading me, I felt as though I was dancing better than I'd ever done. It was as though just by watching him, I became a better dancer.

Or maybe it was that looking at David made me feel so happy inside. There was something about him that made me feel wonderful and I didn't know what it was but all the same, I felt it.

The major problem with fast dancing is that it makes conversation impossible. I mean, there we'd be, face-to-face, our noses almost touching, and I'd start to say something, and then the next step would bounce us in opposite directions and I'd find myself shouting into the startled face of some other dancer.

Laughing, David leaned toward me and put his hands on my shoulders to keep us in line with each other. "Hard place to carry on an intimate conversation," he said.

"How intimate you want to get?" I teased.

His eyebrows shot up with such surprise that without giving my action any thought, I stretched forward and gave him a quick kiss on the cheek.

His grin widened and his eyebrows went up even further.

As David's hands dropped from my shoulders and we swung shoulder to shoulder facing the same direction, there I was staring straight into Rick's narrowed eyes.

His glance raked over both of us. In a low voice that we could both hear clearly but that did not carry beyond us, Rick said, "Two can play that game, my girl."

Then he turned away to pull Leanne into his arms.

I felt stunned.

David kept on dancing, as though nothing had happened, leading me through the crowd away from Rick. We circled each other a few times before he again put his hand on my shoulder and leaned over to say, "Who was that?"

I shrugged and said, "Just a dumb guy I used to date."

Until I said it, I'd thought of Rick as the love of my life. But when I put it into words, I realized that he was no such thing, he was simply a guy I'd once been stupid about and no longer cared for at all.

Rick was exactly what my friends had been telling

me he was. He was selfish and bad-tempered. Maybe with some other girl who didn't treat him like a TV star he would be a nicer person, but I'd been so in love with his looks, I'd never thought about him as a real person. I expected other people to be nice. If they weren't, I didn't waste time with them. But I'd let Rick treat me badly.

As all these thoughts dashed around in my head, I went right on dancing and smiling at David. And then I couldn't think about anything but David. I watched the way he moved and the way he laughed and the way his face lit up when he looked at me. And I wished I'd met him my first day at the U., so that we would have had all these past months together. And then I was glad I hadn't met him back in September, because now it was spring and spring is the perfect time to fall in love and the more I watched David and listened to David, the more I knew that that was exactly what was happening, I was falling crazy in love with this darling guy.

During a break in the music, when we were standing in the crowd, not talking, just looking at each other—because all of a sudden that's all I wanted to do, just look at David—someone said very clearly, "Good for you, Greta." For a minute I didn't hear, but when I did realize what he'd said, I looked around and saw Jon walking past.

David glanced at Jon and then back at me, but he didn't ask me who Jon was. I liked that. It was nice to be with a guy who didn't ask me to explain everyone who spoke to me.

The crepe paper ceiling wavered above us in the fading evening light, a flickering rainbow sky. As the lounge darkened, the lamps were turned on low.

"It's kind of warm in here," David said.

"Uh-huh," I said, knowing exactly what he wanted to do. As I followed him across the dance floor to the patio doors, we passed Inger, dancing with some guy I didn't know.

She peered over his shoulder at me and said, "Way to go."

I winked back.

David had turned to see if I was still behind him. He gave Inger a vague smile, caught my hand and led me outside. I didn't know what he thought Inger meant and I hoped he wouldn't ask. She was referring to me taking her advice, bringing another guy to the dance, but I certainly didn't intend to explain that to David.

Outside the air was all April lovely, like the touch of velvet, with stars everywhere in the night sky. We wandered across the patio and beyond, onto the grass, and David continued his quick, light dance steps and I continued to imitate him.

We danced our way all around Smith Hall, up the path to the main walk, past the grove of alders, right up to the Student Union, until we couldn't hear the April Fool Party band anymore. We danced around the fountain, with its empty pool, and circled the walk lamps, and even danced up the wide stone steps to the main entrance, and at that point we could hear the music from the rec room, very faintly, but enough to pick up its beat.

We held onto each other's hands and danced around each other from one end of the wide landing to the other, until we were both so out of breath, we slowed down, leaned into each other's arms and started laughing. Trying to laugh and catch your breath at the same time isn't easy, so it was a good thing we were hanging on to each other. Otherwise we might have fallen over.

I must admit that that wasn't the main reason I was glad we were hanging on to each other. One thing I know about guys, if you want one to kiss you, he's a lot more apt to do that if he already has his arms around you. And I really wanted David to kiss me.

I could have kissed him first, but as I'd already given him a quick kiss in the lounge, and I didn't want him to think I was chasing him—though by that time, I was—I waited. It couldn't have been more than a few seconds, but I did have this panicky moment when I actually wondered if he was going to step back from me and suggest that we get back to the party.

And then he settled all my worries by going ahead and kissing me. The way his heart was pounding against me, I knew he wasn't kissing me simply because he thought I expected him to, either. For sure he'd been wanting to kiss me for quite a while before he finally got around to it.

It was the perfect way to fall in love, under a starlit sky on a warm spring night.

10

The party never had a formal ending.

It kind of dwindled down. The food ran out. And then the soft drinks. And then the band packed up and left.

But as everyone lived on campus and no one had to be home by any time, Lynne Belmont and her boyfriend, Scotty, set up the sound system, playing people's favorite cassettes. Couples kept wandering in and out of the lounge, some dancing on the patio, others gathering in groups with friends.

And then people began to drift off and disappear, until there were only a few of us left. Finally, though I hated to say it, I whispered to David, "You suppose the party is over?"

We were dancing on the grass at the edge of the patio. The charade players were gone, along with the discussion groups and almost everyone else. I had my arms around David's neck and he had his arms around my waist.

He whispered back, his mouth against my ear, "The music stopped about ten minutes ago. Is that a sign?"

"Did it really?"

"Uh-huh."

We talked about that, still holding on to each other. I said, "I hate for parties to end."

David said, "Don't look at this as an end, think of it as an intermission."

"How long an intermission?"

"Umm, I don't suppose I'll be up too early tomorrow, so say, until tomorrow afternoon?"

"I think we're supposed to clean up the lounge tomorrow afternoon," I said.

"What time?" he asked.

"I don't know."

"Well, when you find out, call me. I could always come help."

We let it go there, definitely agreeing to meet at some vague future time. There were no doubts in my mind. None at all. I was in love with this guy. And if he wasn't in love yet, he soon would be. And then we'd be happily ever after. Who knew more about boys than me? And David had "falling in love" written all over him.

After we'd said our good-byes for the fifth time, I floated up the stairs and drifted down the hallway to my room, daydreaming about David. And what we'd do together tomorrow and the next day and so on after that.

The hallway was spooky, it was so quiet and empty.

When I opened the door to my room, I could see that Marci was already in bed asleep. Reaching around the door without turning on the lights, I grabbed my robe and towel and headed for the bathroom. When I returned, I dropped my clothes in a corner and tiptoed through the dark to my bed.

I didn't notice the time. But it must have been late. As excited as I was, I thought I'd never fall asleep, and yet, I must have been exhausted, too, because the next thing I knew, there was light filtering in around the window blinds.

Pulling my covers over my head, I went back to sleep. Later, I woke, not enough to open my eyes, but enough to tune into the dorm's hall noises. People were running up and down, slamming doors, shouting good mornings, shushing the shouters. I spent a long time wondering whether it was still early or way past time to get up. Should I push back the covers and check my clock? If Marci was awake, she would see me. She wouldn't actually say I should get up, but she might ask if I was ever planning to do so, and there I'd be, faced with a decision.

I listened. I couldn't hear so much as an indrawn breath. Slowly I opened my eyes and even more slowly I pushed back the covers and started to rise to peer at my clock.

And then this terrible thing happened. Maybe terrible isn't the right word. But I don't know the right word.

What happened was I woke up in the wrong room.

And it wasn't even a room I'd ever seen. It wasn't the room of one of my friends. Certainly it was in Smith Hall, I knew that from the hall sounds and the familiar molding around the ceiling and probably mostly from instinct. But where in Smith?

I did not pinch myself to see if I was dreaming. knew clearly that I was awake. And I did not blink in some wild hope that the strange room would go away. I simply stared.

Above me the wall was pink, baby pink, and hanging on it were posters on pink mats. The pictures on the posters were as un-Frazetta as was possible, glossy prints of roses and other pink flowers.

I lowered my gaze to the covers around which my curled fingers were now frozen.

The bedspread was chenille. Pink chenille. The sort of thing my Great-Aunt Millie had in her guest room. The sheet was flowered pink. With a lace edge.

I sat up slowly. I was really terrified as well as unbelieving. How could I possibly have gone to bed in the wrong room? Also, there were some things about it that weren't wrong. It was the right size, the windows were the right shape, the blinds were torn in exactly the same place as my blinds, and the furniture was arranged the same. But of course, all the rooms were about the same size and had the same kind of furniture. But the tear in the blind? What had happened to me last night? Did falling in love leave one totally demented?

The empty bed on the opposite wall, which had always been covered with Marci's dark quilt, was hidden beneath a pink quilt with a ruffled flounce. And above it, on the pink wall, hung not Marci's theater posters, but posters of kittens, all on pink backgrounds.

I almost flung back the covers and dashed into the hall in my pajamas. Almost, but not quite, because as I swung my feet toward the floor, my gaze crossed my dresser top and it *was* my dresser top.

Reflected neatly in the mirror was my row of glass bottles of cologne and nail polish and bath oil and shampoo. No one could have a duplicate collection arranged in the same way, could they? Still doubting my mind, I groped for moral support, honestly questioning my sanity because how clearly can one think first thing in the morning before a shower or breakfast and after a very late party date with a dream of a guy? But I hung in there, looking slowly around, and I saw my own clock and my notebook on the desk, and Marci's typewriter on her desk, and that was Marci's row of books plus one cactus in a clay pot on her shelf.

And then I saw my open closet door. If I'd been in shock before, now I almost died. The whole length of the rod was filled with neatly hung pink clothes. All pink. One hundred percent pink. I jumped up and ran to the closet and started pulling them out, examining them, looking for labels, wondering what size they were and what they were doing in my closet.

Freaking out is one of those things people forever say they're doing when all they're doing is feeling a little crazy, but this time, believe me, I was way past crazy and practically to basket case and on the brink of a personal demonstration of freaking out.

And then it hit me.

I went over to the walls and ran my hand across all that pink. It wasn't wall at all, not painted plaster wall. It was pink bed sheets, carefully tacked up to cover my walls. And between the pink spread and the flowered sheet was my own gold blanket. And inside the flowered case was my pillow.

I let out a shriek and threw open the hall door.

The whole dormitory wing must have been waiting since sunrise for me to wake up. As soon as I opened the door, they burst into laughter.

I stared at them, my mouth hanging open.

In chorus, they shouted, "April Fool!"

And then it all fell in place, the way Inger and Allison teased me about my jungle pastels. The way Marci had hurried me to get down to the party. The running and whispering in the hall the previous day. The way Allison had slammed her door practically in my face.

They must have been collecting pink stuff all week, getting ready to pull off this joke.

And they must have had quite a crew, to completely redo our room in such a short time, because they'd all been at the party.

I looked at them and then I looked back at my room and then I started to laugh, and the more I thought about them racing back and forth, lugging sheets and clothes and posters, probably stationing someone to watch for me to be sure I didn't return to my room during the evening, the funnier it got. And I couldn't stop laughing.

I leaned against the wall, slid down it, sat on the floor and laughed until my sides ached and the tears ran down my face.

And so did everyone else.

If a stranger had walked into the hall, she'd have thought we were a genuine case of mass hysteria.

When we could breathe and talk and move again, which was a long time later, the girls removed all the pink stuff, collected from everyone's rooms, and returned my things.

"How could you do that and keep so quiet about it?" I asked Marci after the others had left.

She giggled, which was very un-Marci. "I didn't know if I could, but as soon as Inger told me about it, I knew it was worth a try."

"So this was Inger's bright idea."

"Umm."

"Did David know about it?" I asked, wondering if they'd told him to keep me busy and away from my room. I had this sinking feeling that maybe all that dancing around the fountain was part of Inger's plan.

"David? No. None of us had met David until last night. He seems like a really nice guy."

"He is and I can hardly wait to tell him," I said. "About the joke, I mean. He'll love it."

Marci nodded and asked if I was going to Sunday brunch at the cafeteria. I told her I was, but probably with David and that I wanted to phone him first. She said fine, she'd see me later. Grabbing her billfold, she jammed it in the back pocket of her jeans, and left to go to the cafeteria.

She was barely out the door when the phone rang. I grabbed it off the hook and almost said, Hi, David, but didn't quite because Marci had stopped in the hallway and was looking at me and I realized she might be expecting Steve to call.

So all I said was hello and then Rick's voice said, "Morning, darling."

Once I would have fallen apart at that deep voice calling me darling. Now all I felt was annoyance that it wasn't David. I wanted Rick off the line so that David could phone.

Shaking my head at Marci so that she'd know it wasn't for her, I said a flat, "Good morning."

Marci waved and left.

Rick said, "Have a big time last night?"

I said, "Yes."

He laughed in that low, short way of his. "Good for you. And now are you done playing games?"

"What's that mean?" I asked.

"Meet me at the cafeteria and I'll tell you."

"Sorry, I'm busy," I said.

"Still mad about Leanne?"

"Leanne has nothing to do with it."

"No, she doesn't," he agreed. "You know I only went out with her for the same reason you were with that guy."

I waited for him to explain further, but being Rick, he stopped there, expecting me to rush in with understanding and apologies. And once I would have done that. But now I didn't. Sure, I knew what he was trying to say, only I didn't care.

Finally he said, "Greta, I don't want to play a lot of dumb games to make each other jealous."

I knew from that that he had lost interest in Leanne and wanted me back. I also knew him well enough to know he'd keep calling unless I made very clear my feelings about him.

That's why I said bluntly, even though blunt isn't usually my style with guys, "Rick, it's over."

"What's over?"

"You and me."

"Still mad, huh?"

"No," I said slowly, "I am not mad at you. I like you, you're a nice guy, but you're not right for me and I don't want to go out with you anymore."

I'd never burned my bridges that way in my life. I mean, keeping ex-boyfriends as friends is one of those things I believe in because who knows when you'll need an old friend? I held my breath, half expecting him to start shouting at me.

Instead there was this long, awful silence, and then he hung up. Didn't say good-bye or anything, just hung up.

I had this fantastic it's-over-and-I-made-it feeling, like I'd aced a major exam, only more so. I let out my breath. My shoulders relaxed. I felt like inviting the whole world to a party to celebrate.

Instead I phoned David. He'd love the April Fool joke. I could hardly wait to tell him about all those pink sheets tacked to my walls. In my imagination I could see his grin widen and his face light up.

He answered and said hi and I said hi and then I said, "Want to meet me for brunch?"

Instead of saying sure, he hesitated, and then he said slowly, "I'm sorry, I guess not today."

"Not today?"

"No, I—I forgot, I've got something I have to do."

There wasn't any sunshine in his voice. The flat tone came through to me. But I didn't want to believe it.

"You're busy all day?" I asked incredulously.

"Uh—I think so."

"Well—shall I call you later?" If I hadn't been so sure of how he felt about me, I'd have thought he was trying to get rid of me.

"Uh—I don't think I'll be here."

He *was* trying to get rid of me! Now I knew how Rick felt. Rick was as sure of me as I was of David. No wonder he had trouble believing me when I said I didn't want to see him again. I couldn't believe that was what David meant. And yet, that's what his tone of voice and his evasive answers were saying.

Had he gone home and thought about me and decided that the whole evening had been a mistake, that I wasn't his kind of girl after all?

Or had I misread him completely? Was he really a guy who naturally poured on the charm with any girl, without meaning a word of it?

Could I be that wrong about guys?

My voice stuck in my throat. I forced it out and to me it sounded more like croaking than speaking, but I managed to say, "See you around later, then," which meant nothing at all.

And David said, "Okay," in that quiet tone and then we hung up.

Why had I ever thought I knew anything about boys?

I knew nothing! I was the dumbest girl at the U.! Joanne, who was still in high school, knew more about boys than I did! She at least knew when a guy wasn't interested in her. I didn't have that much common sense. I'd been spinning around in my daydreams thinking this darling boy was either madly in love with me or well on the way in that direction and definitely past any point of changing his mind. I'd thought I'd finally found the perfect guy for me.

I'd seen all the signs in his words, his actions, his face. It was like going step by step through one of those magazine articles on dating and falling in love, and we'd progressed from A to B to C as neatly as the examples in the articles.

Could all those experts be wrong?

Could my heart be wrong?

Biting back tears, I rummaged through my desk searching for David's sketches. By the time I found them, my nose was running as well as my eyes. I pushed up the window and leaned out, planning to rip the pictures into tiny bits and let them flutter like blossoms through the air. I needed something symbolic to convince myself that love is a rotten lie. I wanted to make a farewell gesture.

The April morning lifted my hair with light breezes, swirling it into my wet eyes. The trees and grass shimmered in the sunlight. People strolled by on the paths, laughing.

I drew back into my room and took a last look at those sketches. The skunk cabbage was as charming as the morning. The picture of me, overwhelmed by books, was done with such care, I couldn't believe it had been drawn by someone who thought of me as nothing special, just another girl. And the picture of David, well, that one about tore me apart. It was done quickly, carelessly, in contrast to the one of me, done as though he'd dashed it off in place of writing a note and had only accidentally drawn that funny line that so perfectly captured his wide smile.

I couldn't tear them up, those three sketches. Maybe sometime when I was an old lady and my heart had healed, but not now.

After putting them carefully back in my desk, I wiped my eyes dry on the hem of my T-shirt and headed out of Smith Hall.

What I wanted to avoid was running into any of my friends. They'd ask what I'd thought of the party and if I'd had a nice time, and they'd tell me about their evenings, and either way, I'd probably fall apart and burst into tears again.

The cafeteria would be as bad, full of people I

knew. Or they might be in the library or sitting on the lawns or wandering down any of the paths.

I had to find someplace where none of them hung out.

And then I thought of the clearing past the bridge and above the stream, the patch of grass by the tree that couldn't be seen from the paths. Maybe if I sat there by myself I could sort out what had happened. Not that I expected to make sense of it, but at least maybe I could get myself calmed down to the point where I could accept the idea that David really did not care for me.

Turning off the bridge through the ferns, I slipped out of my shoes and walked slowly along the stream's mossy bank. The cold dampness oozed through my toes. The sun shone in my eyes.

I turned up the bank toward the clearing.

David was sitting there, his sketchbook in his hand, looking as startled as I felt.

I stood with my mouth open.

He recovered first and said, "Hi."

I blurted, "You want me to go away?"

"Should I?" he asked.

He said it as pleasantly as if we were either on the best of terms or were strangers who had no reason to be rude to each other, I didn't know which.

And I couldn't think. My mind was so muddled. Probably there were dozens of answers to give him that would have been right. Probably I could have told Allison exactly what to say in a similar situation. Probably tomorrow I'd know what I should have said.

But right then, I forgot about tact and charm and snapped, "I don't want your nice lies!"

His eyebrows shot up. "Lies? What lies?"

His behavior had been a lie, but how could I explain that? He'd say it was my fault if I'd misunderstood the way he acted, wouldn't he, wouldn't any guy?

The sun felt burning hot on my face. Or maybe it was my face that was burning hot, all by itself with no help from the sun. I didn't know how to explain, so I blurted, "Maybe you didn't lie, but you weren't exactly honest!"

"When?"

"Last night."

"Last night?" He looked at me for this long, uncomfortable moment. "You want honesty? All right. Honesty is that I don't like to be used to make someone else jealous."

"What!"

"I guess I'm pretty stupid but I'm not deaf. This morning I heard some people in the coffee shop talking about the party last night. I wasn't paying any attention, really, because I was just having coffee and doughnuts to kill time. I woke up really early, see, and so then I was afraid you'd be asleep still and I couldn't think what else to do until it was late enough to phone you. And then while I was thinking about you, somebody said your name, so of course I listened and they said who was the guy you'd been with and someone else said probably some guy to make Rick jealous and someone else said you two were always doing that to each other."

"And you believed that?" I asked.

"I didn't even know who Rick was, but there I was sitting alone with nothing else to think about and then I remembered that guy saying something about two could play games, and it all fell in place, the other guy who said 'Good for you' and Inger making some remark about 'Way to go' and I didn't know what to think."

"You believed it," I said, accusing him with my voice, because I wanted David to be perfect and perfect people don't believe rumors.

"I didn't want to, but I figured I'd better have some time to think about it."

He was not perfect. He had a rotten flaw.

Because of that flaw, he'd come here by himself, probably feeling as unhappy as I did. And I couldn't stand to see David unhappy.

Now if there's one thing I know about boys— and I was beginning to doubt that there was—but if there was, it was that they don't like to be rushed. They like to do the rushing. They want to be the first to fall in love, because if it happens the other way around, they feel trapped. Telling a guy you're crazy about him before he's told you is the sure way to scare a guy off. Everyone knows that.

But I couldn't stop myself. I blurted out, "You want honesty? Honesty is that I am not absolutely sure how I feel about you, but I have this growing suspicion that I am falling madly in love with you."

At that point, according to all I'd ever read, David should have told me that I was a nice girl and he valued my friendship but that he wasn't ready for any serious commitment.

Instead he stood up and walked down the slope to me and kept getting nearer and nearer while I stood there with my heart pounding away in my ears and finally he was right there putting his arms around me.

He said, "I love you, too, Greta."

Which all goes to prove that when it comes right down to basic facts, I don't know the first thing about boys.

#2 THE SHADOWED PATH
Barbara Corcoran

Sixteen-year-old Phyllis Donahue is alone in her family's remote cabin in the Maine woods. But she is not on her own for long—Ron Harrison, a sophisticated young man, is staying in the next cabin; and strong, quiet David Clark, from a nearby town, promises to visit every day. Phyllis's summer seems to be getting better and better. But then she makes an unsettling discovery, and her isolation develops an undertone of terror. Ron is a tantalizing older boy and something of a "dangerous love." David makes Phyllis feel good inside, but she's not sure he cares. Ron is clearly hiding something, and Phyllis may be playing with fire!

#3 DANGEROUS BEAT
Charlotte Flynn

Seventeen-year-old Jennifer Taggert is thrilled to land a summer job helping the music critic of her town's newspaper. When she meets two attractive, but very different boys, she feels luckier than ever. Billy is the outgoing, adorable blond manager of the local rock-'n-roll group. Ken is moody and distant, but Jennifer is strongly drawn to him. Then important review albums start to disappear at work, and Jennifer realizes that someone is trying to get her fired. She *has* to find out who's causing the trouble, and in the process she comes across a mysterious ice house in the woods, an unexplained death, and a possible rival for Ken's affections. She is determined to pursue the mystery to its end—even if it means losing both boys and endangering her life.

**Look for MOONSTONE novels
at your local bookstore!**